Martha Burr Banks

Heroes of the South Seas

Martha Burr Banks

Heroes of the South Seas

ISBN/EAN: 9783741187056

Manufactured in Europe, USA, Canada, Australia, Japa

Cover: Foto ©Andreas Hilbeck / pixelio.de

Manufactured and distributed by brebook publishing software
(www.brebook.com)

Martha Burr Banks

Heroes of the South Seas

Heroes of the South Seas.

BY

MARTHA BURR BANKS,

AUTHOR OF "THE CHILDREN'S SUMMER," "RICHARD AND ROBIN,"
ETC.

YOUNG PEOPLE'S MISSIONARY MOVEMENT
NEW YORK

CONTENTS.

---·◈·---

4

PREFACE.

FOR the material found in this volume the writer is indebted to "The Encyclopædia of Missions," "The Cyclopædia of Missions," "Mission Stories of Many Lands," "The Missionary Review of the World," "The Gospel in All Lands," "The Life of John Williams," "The Life of John Coleridge Patteson," "The Life of John Geddie," "Life of John G. Paton," "Life of James Calvert," "Life of James Chalmers," and several small books, magazines and papers.

Heroes of the South Seas.

CHAPTER I.

ALMOST everybody has heard of Captain Cook, the famous old navigator who used to go cruising round the world, hunting up all sorts of queer places and queer people and opening the way for other explorers. It was in the year 1769, on one of his voyages, that he came across two neighboring groups of islands in the Southern Pacific, one of which had been first seen by an Englishman through the eyes of Captain Wallis, who called it the Georgian Group, after King George of England. Captain Cook, however, did not stop to draw distinctions, but gave the whole cluster the name of the Society Islands, in honor of the Royal Society of London, and though for a while the two groups were commonly known as the Windward and the Leeward Islands they are now both included under the title bestowed upon them by Captain Cook.

The largest island, Tahiti, has a circuit of
one hundred and forty miles, and contains about
six hundred square miles.   It is made up of two
rounded peninsulas joined by a narrow isthmus,
and is crowned by a high mountain peak called
The Diadem. The inhabitants were found to be
tall and stout, with brown skin and dark eyes,
and they seemed merry and good-natured ; but
underneath they were very bad indeed, and
thought nothing of stealing, or of telling lies,
or even of killing anybody with whom they
happened to be vexed, or whom they wished to
put out of the way.

In 1772 the Spaniards tried to settle upon
Tahiti, and when Captain Cook again visited
the islands, in 1777, he saw that they had left
behind them some traces of their religion, for
a house and a cross that had been set up by
them were still carefully kept by the natives.
Then about eleven years passed away, and nothing was heard of the Society Islands until at
last the good ship " Bounty " touched at those
shores for the purpose of obtaining a supply of
the plants of the breadfruit tree to transport to
the British West Indies.

The story brought back by the crew of this
vessel, together with the former accounts of the
island presented by Capt. Cook, roused so much
interest in England that the London Missionary

Society was formed in order that a ship might
be fitted out to carry the gospel to those be-
nighted people in the South Seas. Thirty men
came forward who were willing to be the bearers
of the glad tidings, and Capt. Wilson, who had
retired from the East India service and was now
living in wealth and ease at home, volunteered
to take charge of the missionary ship, which had
been named the Duff.   Four of the messengers
were ministers and the rest were tradesmen.
The ensign of the ship was a purple flag, having
three doves bearing olive-branches as its device ;
and as the banner fluttered in the wind and the
vessel rode out of the harbor, on the 10th of August, 1796, the little band broke out into the
hymn, " Jesus, at thy command we launch into
the deep ;" and so they sailed away, strong,
firm, brave, and true, hoping to do some of the
wonderful kind of fishing taught to mankind
long ago by the Sea of Galilee.

It took seven months for the Duff to weather
the gales and make the voyage to Tahiti, but
the strangers received a warm welcome when
they arrived.

Seventy-five canoes came out to meet them,
and the natives clambered over the sides of the
vessel with many signs of joy, probably promising themselves, down in their crafty hearts, that
they could soon barter some of the pigs and the

fruit that they had brought with them for those valuable knives and axes, and other things, that white men usually had about them. But the day was Sunday, and the new-comers would have nothing to do with bargains just then ; but, as some of the men were willing to stay with them, even though there was no prospect of trading, they held a service on board the ship, and the natives looked on in wonder while the missionaries prayed and sang.

When the white men went on shore one of the chiefs showed them an empty house, about one hundred feet long, where he said they might live ; so they at once took possession of their new home, and hallowed it by a little service within its walls that same night. On Sunday they preached to the people, having for an interpreter a white man who had been at some time cast upon the island and who had become very much like the natives. The following Sunday Pomare, the father of the ruling king, came to the meeting. In Tahiti, so soon as a son is born into the royal family he is acknowledged as the sovereign, and the former king loses his authority. Pomare had been the supreme chief of the island, and he was supposed to be very wise, but his wisdom could not equal his wickedness had he had even more knowledge than was credited to him.

There were other queer customs on that island of Tahiti. The king and queen rode on the shoulders of men, and never touched their feet to the ground, because whatever they stood on became at once their property. When the attendants who carried them were exchanged for others the royal beings were obliged to jump over the heads of the first men to the shoulders of the second set. They would not go on board of the ship, for the reason that the vessel would then belong to them, and they warned their new friends not to hold an umbrella over their heads as that, too, would immediately become theirs.

There were, besides, on these islands, some strange people who were called dancers. They blackened their bodies with charcoal and dyed their faces red. Their only business in life was to kill people, and their only amusements were dancing, boxing and wrestling.

The favorite god, whose name was Oro, was nothing but a log of wood about as large as a man. It was kept in a shed among a grove of trees surrounded by a stone wall. The priests would roll themselves up in bundles of cloth, and by disguising their voices pretend to be speaking for the gods; and though the people were not really deceived they dared not disobey the commands of the priests. There were many other idols. Some were made of stone, but most of them were of wood, and there were more than one hundred kinds. Some of the gods were supposed to protect thieves, some cared for murderers, and most of them demanded human sacrifices. There were numerous superstitions, too. One of them was a strong belief in the power of red feathers; and the people were sure that they never could have any success in fishing unless they carried a bunch of scarlet feathers with them when they went out upon the water.

In this difficult place, among these ignorant, degraded people, the good men from over the sea settled down and went to work in earnest to do what they could to lift them from their low condition; but the task was even harder than had been expected. When the missionaries were abused, if they did not revenge themselves, they were despised as cowards; but they made up their minds that they would defend themselves only when necessary, and would trust in God and try to win their way by kindness and patience. They started a hospital, but the suspicious people would have nothing to do with it. They seemed to care little for the new teachings and were deeply offended if any of their evil customs were rebuked.

But, after three years of labor, a Christian chapel was built, and in 1800 eight new mission-

COCOANUT PLANTATION, RAIATEA, SOCIETY ISLANDS.

aries came to the rescue. Among them was
Henry Nott, who proved himself one of the
best of the missionaries to the South Seas. Mr.
Nott and one of his companions made a tour
round the island and preached everywhere.
Sometimes they preached two or three times a
day, and all the time the missionaries prayed
with all their hearts that they might bring a
blessing to these poor people whom they had
come to help.

But still the wars and the wickedness went
on, and the natives would answer all the per-
suasions of their friends to leave their old ways,
and take hold of better things, with the words:
" None of the chiefs believe you, so why should
we?"

In 1803 the old king died, and his son took
the name of Pomare Second. He had learned
to read and write, and the people were much
afraid of him. They believed that he had
gained power by which he could kill a man just
by prayers and charms. The missionaries then
turned their attention towards the children. One
of them opened a school in his own home, and
taught reading and writing to the girls and boys
by making letters in the sand. He also wrote
some books, and sent them to England to be
printed; but it was hard to put Christian ideas
into a language in which there was no word for

God, and no way by which the thought of gratitude might be expressed.

In 1807 another war broke out, and all the
missionaries had to flee from Tahiti. The king
took refuge in the island of Eimeo, not far away,
and after a while invited the missionaries to follow him to that place. They were ready to go
anywhere if only there was a chance of doing
good. So over to Eimeo they moved, from the
island in which they had sought shelter, and
there they built a chapel and started a school.
Before long they noticed that the king seemed
to be losing a little of his old faith in idols and
superstitions. A sacred turtle was caught one
day, and, instead of sending it to the temple,
as was the custom in such cases, he was bold
enough to have it cooked, and then ate it with
much enjoyment. As no harm came to him in
consequence of this meal, his confidence in his
gods was still more shaken. Then further encouragement came to the missionaries: Pomare
really asked to be baptized. They thought it
would be better to wait a while before granting
his request, so that they might be sure that he
was sincere in his profession that he meant to
take Jehovah as his God; but when they saw
that he was truly sorry for his past wickedness,
and that he was careful about keeping Sunday
in the Christian way and was doing his best to

persuade his subjects to give up their idols and
to worship the true God, they could not doubt
his earnestness.

For nearly sixteen years now they had been
working in these islands, and this was about all
the fruit they had gathered so far.   Some of
them began to feel that, like Peter and his companions on the little lake in Palestine, they had
toiled all the night and taken nothing.   Even the
London Missionary Society had almost decided
to give up the work as hopeless.   But there
were one or two men who had not come to the
end of their faith yet.   One of them said that
he would sell the clothes from his back before
he would let go of the scheme, and he proposed
that instead of sitting down in despair they
should fall to praying harder than ever for this
poor, disheartening little mission.   To this the
others agreed, and while the men in the Pacific
labored the men at home prayed.

Now just about this time Pomare was invited
to go back to Tahiti, and the missionaries at
Eimeo heard a rumor that the people there
were beginning to wake up and to think a little
about what had been told them by those strangers whom they had driven away.   At this
report, two of the exiles hurried back to Tahiti
to see if the good news were true.   They found
out that two of their old servants who had been

left behind had been influenced by the words and the lives of their masters almost without knowing the fact themselves, and since their departure these men had been praying together, as well as they knew how, and had persuaded others to join them in this practice. They had, too, made up their minds to give up their idols, to keep Sunday as a day of rest, and to worship only Jehovah. The way was wide open for the missionaries and their message.

Mr. Nott gathered a crowd of savages in one of the cocoanut groves of Tahiti, and told them the beautiful, wonderful old story to which they would not listen before. As he was reading the sixteenth verse of the third chapter of John, one chief cried out, "Will you read that again?" Slowly and carefully Mr. Nott read over the words once more: "For God so loved the world that he gave his only begotten Son, that whosoever believeth in him should not perish, but have everlasting life." The man listened eagerly. "Does that mean Tahiti?" he asked.

"Yes," said Mr. Nott, pointing his finger straight at the dusky figure before him, "it means *you*." The chief took the answer in simple faith, and became himself, in course of time, a devoted missionary to his people. The men who were praying at home had their reward, too. The ship from London, carrying letters of cheer and hope to the missionaries in Eimeo, was met in mid-ocean by the vessel bearing the news of the overthrow of idolatry in Tahiti, and loaded with a cargo of the rejected idols. So the night of toil was lightened by the breaking of the dawn, and the One who had come to the aid of the weary fishermen in Galilee had given these workers, too, the desire of their hearts.

In 1813 the people in Eimeo also began to throw away their gods of wood and of stone and to bow down to the one God of all mankind. An old priest brought out the idols, one by one tore off their sacred garments, made of finely-braided cloth of cocoanut fibres and ornamented with red feathers, and threw both gods and clothing into the fire, calling to the people to come and see how helpless were the logs that they had worshipped.

King Pomare was not successful in establishing his kingdom again in Tahiti, so he went back to Eimeo, taking with him a large number of followers who called themselves Christians. At Tahiti the native Christians who had been left there were cruelly treated by the remaining heathen, and many ran away to Eimeo. This action brought on a battle between the inhabi-

tants of the two islands, and Pomare came off
victor.   Instead of destroying his enemies, according to the old heathen fashion, he made
away with their idols.   Even that great god Oro
he did not spare, but first disgraced it by standing it up in his kitchen and driving pegs into
it upon which to hang baskets of food, and then
disposed of it altogether by burning it for fuel.

Soon after this occurrence Pomare was re-
stored to his rightful government, and the people themselves cast away the rest of their idols,
pulled down their temples, and began to build
chapels.   Pomare wrote a prayer, which he
often read in these places of worship ; and as for
the missionaries, they could scarcely find time
for rest, as they were so closely followed by
those who had questions to ask, or who were
anxious to learn to read.   In 1816 Pomare collected his own household gods and sent them
to England, so that, as he said, the people there
might see the foolish idols that had been so
highly valued in Tahiti.   These idols were
placed in the museum of the London Missionary
Society.

About this time a printing press was brought
to Eimeo, and this fresh wonder caused great
excitement among the natives of the islands.
From far and near they flocked to see the
strange sight, and their canoes lined the shore

while the men were climbing up on one another's shoulders to peer in the windows of the
room in which it had been placed, exclaiming
in astonishment and delight, " O Britain, land
of skill!"   They also brought plantain leaves
to the missionaries, begging that spelling-books
might be written upon them, and when the
Gospel of Luke was completed in the Tahitian
language, and copies were printed, they could
hardly be given out fast enough to the waiting
people.   Then dogs and cats and goats were
killed, so that their skins might be used as
covers for the precious volumes.

It was about 1817 that John Williams, afterwards called "The Apostle of the Pacific,"
landed at Eimeo to put his shoulder to the
wheel with the other men from abroad.   On
the voyage from England he had examined
every part of the vessel on which he sailed, and
the first thing that he did after his arrival was
to complete a boat that had been laid down
three years before.   In ten months he had
learned the language of the island, by moving
freely among the people and chatting with them
on every occasion, thus wiling away from them
their hearts and their speech at the same time.

The missionaries who had fled to Huahine,
in the other group of the Society Islands, at the
time of the trouble in Tahiti, had taught the

natives there something about the gospel, and afterwards, when Pomare was at war with Tahiti, several ships from those islands had gone over to assist him to regain his throne, and had carried home with them a little more truth. Tamatoa, the king of Raiatea, had been especially impressed with the results that came from the Christian religion.

On his return to his own island, when he saw the crowds on the shore waiting to welcome him with joy, and evidently expecting him to bring with him many war captives, he placed a herald in the front of his canoe and told him to shout to the people, "We have brought no victims slain in battle. We are all praying people and worship the true God."

Then the books that the missionaries had given him were held up, and the herald cried, "These are the victims, the trophies, with which we have returned!" When Tamatoa landed he gave an account of what he had seen in Tahiti, and about one-third of the people agreed to join him in trying to live in the Christian way. Soon after his arrival Tamatoa fell ill, and one of his friends said that Jehovah must have sent this sickness because he was angry that the great national idol had not been destroyed, and he proposed that it should at once be put out of the way. A brave band went to

the temple, took the god from his seat and set
fire to the building.   The heathen party was
very angry at this deed, and a house of cocoanut
trunks and breadfruit trees was built into which
the Christians were to be thrust and burned alive.
The Christians tried to make peace, but the only
answer that they received was, " There is no
peace for god-burners until they have felt the
effects of the fire that destroyed Oro."   Then
the men who worshipped Jehovah sought his
protection in prayer, and when their enemies
came upon them early in the morning, while
they were still on their knees, they rushed out
and so boldly assailed the invaders that they
departed in haste and alarm.   They expected
to receive the treatment that they had had in
store for the Christians ; but when they were
met with forgiveness and kindness they were
overcome with surprise.   A great feast was
spread for them, at which nearly one hundred
pigs were baked whole, and served with bread-
fruit and other vegetables, but the men were so
humbled and abashed that they could hardly
eat anything.   One man arose and said : " Let
every one eat as he will ; but for my part, never
again, to my dying day, will I worship the gods
that could not protect us in the hour of danger.
We were four times the number of the praying people, yet with the greatest ease they have

conquered us. Jehovah is the true God. Had
we been conquerers they would now be burning
in the house we made for the purpose; but instead of injuring us, or our wives or children,
they have set for us this sumptuous feast.
Theirs is a religion of mercy. I will go and
join myself to this people."

That same night every one of the heathen
party bowed in prayer to Jehovah, and all gave
thanks for their own defeat. The next morning
both parties worked together in destroying every
idol and temple in the island, and in a small
one near by as well; and in three days after this
time not a remnant of idolatry could be found
in either place. Huahine, Borabora and Maurea,
other islands of the group, began to follow the
example of the people of Raiatea; and two men
from Huahine were sent to Tahiti to ask for
teachers. John Williams, William Ellis, and one
other missionary answered this call, and in 1818
they went over to Huahine. Then Tamatoa
begged for a missionary of his own, and John
Williams finally settled at Raiatea.

In 1819 the Royal Mission Chapel in Tahiti
was finished. It was two hundred and twelve
feet longer than St. Paul's in London, and contained one hundred and three windows and
twenty-nine doors. It was so large that no
preacher could be heard throughout the whole

building, so three pulpits were placed within it, at suitable distances apart, and three ministers preached at once to a congregation of six thousand people.

After the dedication of the chapel laws were published, forbidding murder, theft, Sabbath-breaking, and other things, and when the king asked his chiefs if they would agree to these rules even the one who had been the ringleader among the rebels held up both hands, in token of his wish to be good and obedient.

Pomare died in 1821, and his son, only four years old, was crowned by Mr. Nott. The translation of the whole Bible into Tahitian was completed in 1836, Mr. Nott having done most of the work. The remainder of his life was spent in Tahiti, and in 1844 he died.

In the year 1827 some men were driven from the Pearl Islands to Tahiti on account of war in their own country. These islands are made up of bits of land called Harp Island, Chain Island, Crescent Island and Bow Island, on account of their various shapes. While away from home these people picked up some seeds of gospel truth, and on their return to their friends and relatives they told what they had seen and heard on their voyage, and their story was accepted and acted upon. The idols were cast down, and Jehovah was chosen as the God of the Pearl

Islands too.   From Tahiti and the adjacent islands not less than one hundred and sixty evangelists have gone forth carrying the message of salvation to other tribes.   The spirit that moves in the hearts and lives of these converts, who about a century ago were nothing but savages, is well expressed in their own words.

" Let our hands forget how to lift the club or throw the spear.   Let our guns decay with rust; we do not want them.   Though we have been pierced with bows or spears, if we pierce each other now let it be with the word of God."

The cause of missions has been much hindered by the French occupation of the islands, but the stations are now under the care of the French Protestant Society, and it is hoped that the good work may never be crushed out.   It is said that the natives take much more kindly to the Protestant religion than to that of the Romanists, and that it is wonderful how well they keep to their good principles and their Christian faith when they are surrounded by so many evil influences.

CHAPTER II.

TIIE IIERVEY ISLANDS: A BRAVE DISCOVERER.

WIIEN John Williams went to live in Raiatea he found the people scattered all over the
island in separate villages, so far apart that there
was no chance of helping the inhabitants to work
together in leaving off their old ways and forming new ones, and everybody was jealous and
suspicious of everybody else. The first thing
that he did, therefore, was to form a settlement
where they might live together in comfort,
peace and fellowship. He began by building a
house for himself, so that he might show the natives what a good home should be like and how
it was to be made. This house was sixty feet
long and thirty feet broad, and had seven rooms,
four of which were in front and three behind.
He made also all the furniture of his new dwell-
ing. The men were quick in catching his ideas,
and clever in carrying them out, and at the end
of twelve months the houses extended two miles
along the seashore, and altogether there were
about one thousand people living in them.

Having finished this task, John Williams
made up his mind that he must have a boat,
and he soon had one put together, formed of

planks held in place by the native cord. The natives, though naturally very lazy, set to work to imitate his example ; and while their hands were busy this new comrade of theirs lost no opportunity for teaching them other things besides boat-building, and in his pleasant, friendly way he dropped many a word of that good gospel that would do so much more for them than any other kind of learning. They listened to him readily, and tried to put this part of his teaching into practice. One man used to pray earnestly : "Oh, Jehovah, give thy word into my heart, all thy word, and cover it up there, that it may not be forgotten by me."

There was, too, a poor old cripple who used to sit by the wayside, and when the people were going home from church he would beg them to tell him a little of what they had heard there. "One gives me one piece," he said, "and another another, and I gather them together in my heart; and thinking over what I thus obtain, and praying God to make me know, I get to understand." When he first saw Mr. Williams he said, in greeting, "Welcome, servant of God, who brought light into this dark island. To you we are indebted for the word of heaven."

Some Bibles were sent to the people and they were all anxious to learn to read. Then they wished to have their neighbors share some of the blessings that had come to them. A missionary society was started, which in one year gave about $2,500 for the purpose of "causing the word of God to grow," as they said themselves. Even the king and queen prepared arrow-root with their own hands, as a contribution to this object. "Why," said Tamatoa, the king, "we would not give that to God upon which we bestowed no labor." For some reason these new Christians go far ahead of the old ones sometimes. Perhaps these people had caught the spirit of their leader, John Williams. "Our hearts take in all the ends of the earth," he said, and he found it hard to content himself within the limits of a single reef when there was so much to be done outside of his own little island.

But he did not neglect the work close at hand, in spite of the pulling of his heart-strings in another direction. "I have given myself wholly to the Lord," said he; and his Master's work he could find anywhere.

He built a new chapel for his congregation, setting off part of it for a court-house. Everything about the building astonished the natives, but that which was a special matter for wonder and admiration was that he had contrived a sort of chandelier in which cocoanut shells were used as lamps. The opening day two thousand four hundred persons were present, and the next day a code of laws was adopted and the king's brother was made chief judge of the island.   Then Mr. Williams provided honest employment for the people by beginning the cultivation of the sugar-cane, which grows on the island, and he also put up a sugar-mill for their use.

It was in the spring of the year 1821 that a pestilence broke out in the Austral Islands, about three hundred miles away, south of the Society Islands.   Two chiefs of Rurutu, one of these islands, each built himself a canoe, and then crowding their boats with as many persons as they would hold they set sail upon the broad ocean, not knowing whither they were going. They landed at Raiatea at last, and were much interested in all the new and surprising things that they saw there ; and when they thought it safe to venture back to their own country they begged two of the native teachers to go with them and teach them how to live as Christians. " We cannot go home to our land of darkness without a light in our hands," they said touchingly, and were made very happy by having their petition granted and being able besides to take with them several copies of the gospels in Tahitian, a language something like their own.

" The priests have deceived us," they told their friends on their return ; and in order to

prove the truth of their words they made a
feast at which they allowed the women to eat
some of the things that were usually forbidden
to them. As these women did not fall down
and die on the spot, or have any other dreadful
thing happen to them, the people believed what
had been told them, and lost no time in pulling
down their temples and burning their altars.
In a few weeks Christianity became the religion
of the island ; the converts sent a load of idols
over to Raiatea, to tell their own story, and then
hastened to spread the light among the other
islands in the same group. These idols were
publicly exhibited in the church at Raiatea.
The national god of Rurutu was called Aa, and
he was the most interesting of all the images,
for he was decked all over outside with little
gods, and in his back was a door, which was
opened and twenty-four small idols were found
hidden away inside of him.

"Ah," said one of the converts at Raiatea,
"angels would rejoice to be employed by God
to teach the world this gospel of Christ."

The missionary society at Raiatea was so
much encouraged by this good piece of work
that its contributions grew to the sum of $9,000.
" A little property given with the heart becomes
big property in the sight of God," one of the
members had said, and all the collections of this

society must have been especially blessed, because all were offered out of pure love and gratitude.

A Christian church was formed at Raiatea now,
and about this time five hundred persons were
baptized. Then John Williams and his wife both
fell ill, partly because they had not proper food,
and they had to take a trip to Australia in search
of a doctor. On their way they stopped at Aitutaki, one of the Hervey or Cook group of islands,
and left there two native teachers among the
savages, who were not pleasant-looking hosts.
They were indeed most hideous to behold, for
their bodies were tattooed all over and smeared
with pipe-clay, red or yellow ochre, or charcoal.

Mr. Williams soon won back his health at
Sydney, and began at once to look round to see
if he could not in some way obtain a ship that he
might use for the purpose of trading from his
islands to New South Wales. The London Missionary Society at first thought the plan a foolish
one, but John Williams was not a man to yield
his point without good reason, so the members
gave in at last to his arguments, and a schooner
was bought for him, and called the Endeavor, a
name that the natives afterwards changed to the
Beginning. Mr. Williams loaded his boat with
shoes, clothing, tea, and other articles, engaged
a man to go with him to teach his people the art

of cultivating sugar and tobacco, and with several sheep and cows as presents from the governor of New South Wales he sailed away
home, having gained more on his voyage than
many persons find on a hunt for health.

Tamatoa, the king, was delighted with the
new ship, and immediately sat down and wrote
a letter of thanks to the directors of the London
Society.

"A ship is good," wrote he, wisely, "for by
its means useful property will come to our lands
and our bodies be covered with decent cloth.
But this is another use of the ship: when we
compassionate the little lands near to us, and
desire to send two among us to those lands to
teach them the gospel of Jesus Christ, the good
word of the kingdom."

Ah, to send on "the good word of the kingdom "—that was what John Williams was all on
fire to do. The teachers left at Aitutaki had, for
a while, had a hard time with their wild pupils.
The savages had laughed at them, calling them
"two logs of driftwood cast up by the sea," and
had not treated them with much courtesy in any
way. But before long the natives became somewhat interested, and would listen to what was
told them about this strange new religion. They
even promised, at last, that if John Williams
would come himself to see them again they

would give up their idols.   Of course, with such
an invitation it did not take much urging to
bring John Williams over the water, for he believed that "a lazy missionary is an ugly and
useless thing," and he could never have too
much of this sort of work to do.   When he
reached Aitutaki the people waded out into the
sea, and crowded round his boat, calling out like
pleased children, "Good is the word of God.   It
is well now with Aitutaki.   The good word has
taken root at Aitutaki."   Then they held up
their hats and their books and said over as
many bits from the Bible as they could remem-
ber, trying to show that they were doing their
best to fall into the new way.   They had built
many houses, and had a neat chapel, which
had been whitewashed by the teachers.   This
work had caused great surprise among the
islanders.   "Just see, they are roasting stones,"
they whispered one to another; and when the
coating was dry they shook their puzzled heads,
and said, solemnly, "The very stones in the sea
and the sand on the shore become good property
in the hands of those who worship the true God
and regard his word."

But Mr. Williams did not end his journey
at Aitutaki, for there he found some natives
from Rarotonga, another of the Hervey Islands.
These men had been driven out of their course

by a gale, and had been thrown upon Aitutaki. There they had become Christians, and now they wished to return and tell the people of Rarotonga the good things that they had learned.

Captain Cook had once been to Rarotonga, and the inhabitants of the island had been interested in the white men, all of whom they called " Kookes," after Captain Cook. Since that time they had been looking out for a second visit from the " Kookes," and now here was a chance to fulfil their expectations, if the white men would go home with the wanderers. There was only one trouble about carrying out this plan, and that was that none of them knew the way. John Williams thought that they might find it together, and here was a little cruise after his own heart ; for to reach new islands was his constant desire and aim. He took the lost mariners on board his ship, and also the king of Aitutaki, and thirty-one of the discarded idols. There went with him besides one of the native teachers, whose name was Papeiha, and who was the kind of Christian that we read about in the Acts of the Apostles, in the days of Paul and Philip and Stephen, and all the rest. Then off they sailed upon their voyage of discovery.

But Rarotonga seemed astray in the ocean,

and nobody knew exactly where to look for it.
The vessel touched at the island of Atui, where
two teachers had been living for two months,
although they had not been very well cared for.
They had often been hungry, and many of their
goods had been stolen from them.   The chief
of the island came on board the ship, and
Papeiha took him down into the hold and
showed him the idols stowed away there, while
Mr. Williams told him what the Bible says about
such gods.   The chief was much impressed, and
the next day declared his intention of throwing
aside his images forever. "Eyes they have, it is
true," he said, " but wood cannot see ; ears they
have, but wood cannot hear."   He then carried
his guests over to two small islands in his kingdom and ordered the people there to cast away
their idols.   These natives were very simple
and ignorant, and willingly obeyed. The goats
that Mr. Williams brought with him they called
"birds with great teeth in their heads."

The chief of these islands told Mr. Williams
that Rarotonga was only a few days' sail distant,
and having learned the direction in which to
steer the party again set forth, although the
natives among them begged that no further
search might be made, as the people of Rarotonga were known to be terrible cannibals.

Still Mr. Williams tried to calm their fears

and pressed on. Five days passed and nothing
came to reward their efforts. At the end of
that time, John Williams, like Columbus before
him, had to promise to turn back if land were
not sighted at a given hour. One half-hour before the close of this period there was a cry
from the man on the look-out, "There is the
island we are seeking !"

There it lay before them—Rarotonga, with
its cruel, wicked inhabitants.

So soon as the ship came into sight thirty or
forty of the savages jumped into their canoes
and went forth to meet the strangers, eager to
see what sort of beings they were. Fortunately
the natives seemed very friendly, and greeted
the new-comers in the best South Sea manner,
by rubbing their noses, which were covered with
cocoanut oil, against those of the missionaries
and teachers. This action, though not very
agreeable, was comforting, for it showed good
feeling ; but the Rarotongans seemed not very
anxious to have any of the visitors go ashore
with them. However, Papeiha made his way to
the land and explained to the people the object
of the expedition. Makea, the king, greeted
him kindly, promised to protect the teachers,
and went on board the ship to conduct them
to the shore. But during the night these
teachers were so badly abused that in the morn-

ing they returned to the boat and were not willing to go back to the island.   Then Papeiha came nobly to the front.   " I will stay here," he said, "if you will send my friend Tiberio to work with me.   I am not afraid.   Whether they spare me or kill me I will land among them. Jehovah is my shepherd ; I am in his hand."

So with only his clothes, his little store of books and his New Testament, Papeiha stepped into a canoe and went over to the shore.   A crowd of warriors gathered upon some rocks that jutted into the water, and as he stepped upon the beach they lifted their spears ready to hurl them at him ; but, either from awe or curiosity, they dropped their arms and let him passed unharmed.   As he walked on towards the house of the chief the people followed him in a body, one crying ; " I 'll have his hat ;" and another, " I 'll take his shirt," and a third, " I shall have his jacket."   But before they could rob him of his clothes they were met by Makea, the king.

"Speak to us, O man," he said to Papeiha, "that we may know the business on which you have come."

" Why," replied Papeiha, " I have come to tell you about my God, and about Jesus Christ, so that you may burn up your idols as the people in all the other islands are doing."

" Burn our gods !" exclaimed the people, in

dismay. "What gods shall we have then, and what shall we do without gods?"

Papeiha did not stop to answer all their questions just then, but day after day, after his companions had left him, he patiently instructed them in the learning of the One who, as he could read in his Gospel of Matthew, had promised to be with his followers always and everywhere.

And that One had been in Rarotonga before him. A heathen woman had already, in some manner, brought a little of the gospel story from Tahiti, so far away. Makea had been interested, and had built an altar to Jehovah; so, like Paul at Athens, Papeiha had only to declare unto the people the Unknown God whom so ignorantly they were worshipping. When Tiberio, the friend of Papeiha, came to Rarotonga, the two men did their best to teach the natives a better religion than they yet knew. One old chief was anxious to learn how to pray, but as the idea of prayer was new to him he was a slow pupil, and poor tired Papeiha would sometimes fall asleep during the lesson. Then the chief would awaken him, saying piteously: "Please go over it again for me, for I have forgotten it."

Papeiha told the people that their idols were not gods, and that the true God was a Spirit, and could not be seen.

"Oh! oh!" cried the excited natives. "Why does he talk like this? Does he think that we are blind? He says that his God cannot be seen; and yet look at him! He carries his God about with him. See how he talks to it, and what his God says to him he tells us. Wherever he goes he carries it; when he sleeps he has it near him. That is his God."

What the people thought was Papeiha's God was simply his little New Testament that he had always near him, and when he was reading it they believed that it was talking to him.

But after a while they began to see things more clearly, and at last one of the priests decided to destroy his idols. He brought his little boy and placed him under the care of the teachers, lest some evil should befall him on account of this daring act, and then went home and came back staggering under the weight of the god he was carrying.

His friends told him that he was a madman, and begged him not to put himself in so much danger, and when a saw was brought out, with which to cut the sacred object to pieces, they all fled in great alarm, thinking that the end of all things had come. But when they saw that the priest went on with his work and then threw the bits of wood into a large fire, where they quietly burned to ashes, and nothing terrible came upon him, they made up their minds that their idols, too, were good for nothing, and should meet the same fate.   In less than ten days fourteen idols were cast into the flames, and then one of the chiefs set fire to the temple. " My heart has taken hold of the word of Jehovah," he said, as a reason for his conduct.

The king himself gave up his faith in his worthless gods, and a small chapel was built for the worship of Jehovah.

Meanwhile Mr. Williams was having his own trials in the island of Raiatea. The London Missionary Society had decided that, after all, the Endeavor was an unnecessary expense, and with much regret Mr. Williams was obliged to part from the little vessel that had been so help-ful to him.   But if he could not go out of Raia-tea he would work the harder there.   He began to translate the Bible into the native tongue, and his wife formed a class for poor, lame, deaf or blind old women, who were neglected by the people.

Then Mr. and Mrs. Pitman came from Eng-land to assist in the labor in Rarotonga.   " If I only had a ship," said Mr. Williams in greeting to these new workers, " not an island in the Pa-cific but I would, with God's will, go to see, and leave teachers there."

But while he was waiting he learned to make

ropes, which he sold to captains of ships. In
1827 he took Mr. Pitman to his field in Rarotonga. He himself expected to come back with the
ship, but it had received damage from a storm,
and the captain felt that he must hasten home
and begin repairs, and could not wait for Mr.
Williams.

John Williams, therefore, took his clothes
and a few other articles on shore, and there he
stayed for twelve months.

His first work was to move the missionary
settlement to a better site, on the other side of
the island. When this was done, he was asked
to seat himself outside of his house, and then
a long train of natives filed past him and laid
their idols at his feet. The smallest of these
images was five feet long and about four inches
in diameter. The next Sunday there was a
congregation of four thousand people, and as
the chapel was too small for the attendance it
was thought best to build a new one. In seven
weeks this house of worship was completed, although five years before not a man on the island
had ever seen an axe or a plane.

While the chapel was building Mr. Williams
made a great stir among the natives by writing
something on a chip and sending it to his wife;
for when it was found that she understood the
message without a word having to be spoken

one of the men caught up the wonderful piece of wood, and holding it high above his head he ran through the village, shouting, "See the wisdom of these English people : they can make chips talk! They can make chips talk!"

Among the queer customs of Rarotonga was one that allowed a son, so soon as he was old enough, to wrestle with his father for the possession of the property. Should he prove the stronger he would turn his parents out and claim the house and farm for his own. If a man died all the relatives could come to his house and take anything they might wish, leaving the widow and children to starve. To do away with these unfair practices Mr. Williams brought out the code of laws used at Raiatea, and it was adopted by the people.

It was not luxurious living on these islands of the Pacific. It was ten years after their arrival before Mr. and Mrs. Williams tasted beef, and then they had lost their relish for it. In Rarotonga they had nothing to eat for weeks except a scanty supply of native roots.

For many months no ship came near the island. But Mr. Williams was as full of devices as was Robinson Crusoe. As he had no boat at hand he would make one to suit himself. He had no knowledge of ship-building, except the little that he had picked up here and there,

and he had few of the necessary tools.   He had
no saw, no oakum, cordage or sail-cloth ; but he
twisted the bark of the hibiscus into ropes,
quilted native mats for sails, and constructed a
rudder out of a piece of a pick-axe, a cooper's
adze and a large hoe.   In five months it was
ready for use.   He called it the Messenger of
Peace, and he made a successful trial trip in
the little vessel to Aitutaki and back.   On his
return he found that his devoted natives had
cleared away all the rubbish left by the building.   "We will not leave a chip against which
he can strike his foot," they said.

Two new missionaries, named Mr. and Mrs.
Buzacott, came to Rarotonga in 1828.   They
set Mr. Williams free to go back to Raiatea, and
when there he offered to lend his new ship to
the London Missionary Society, so that they
might send missionaries to visit the Marquesas
Islands.   Some teachers had been placed upon
these islands by the Duff, on her first voyage,
although they had had but slight encouragement so far.

CHAPTER III.

THE SAMOAN ISLANDS. OVER THE SEA TO SAMOA.

THE following year Mr. Williams went over to Rurutu, where he met a chief from another island who had been waiting two years hoping to take back a teacher to his own land. While away from home his wife and two children had died, but he would not leave the spot until he had accomplished his object.

After John Williams had returned to Raiatea he immediately set about preparations for a voyage to the Samoan Islands, which had not yet been reached by the gospel. This was a plan that he had long had in mind, and now, with the help of the Messenger of Peace, he meant to carry it out. The Samoan Islands were about two thousand miles away, but that fact did not take the courage and the determination out of John Williams. Difficulty and danger seemed only to make him more resolute and more daring.

Before going to Samoa he visited the Hervey Islands, although they were out of his course. He stopped first at Mangaia, to which two teachers had been sent after Mr. Williams' first call at that island five or six years before, and the good missionary was delighted to be welcomed by about five hundred Christians, the results of the work of these men.

These converts had cut off their hair. The heathen wear long hair, but as the Christians wear their hair short it had come to be a kind of first step in giving up heathenism to bring the length of the locks down to that of those of the white men. In speaking of any one who had accepted the Christian religion the natives were wont to say, "Such a one has cut his hair." So John Williams felt sure of the sincerity of the people of Mangaia because they had been willing to make this sacrifice in order to be as much as possible like the Christians.

At Atui, where he next landed, a great advance was seen in all good things. Then he went on to Rarotonga, where he found that during his absence a terrible plague had broken out and nearly six hundred persons had died. Fortunately the missionaries had with them a large supply of medicines, with which they were able to give much relief. Then the Messenger of Peace touched at Aitutaki, where the converts placed in his hands the large sum of $515 for the London Missionary Society. This money had been made by the sale of pigs; each family

having dedicated a pig to the work of "causing the word of God to grow," and these animals had been sold to the crews of the vessels that had come to Aitutaki.

With a happy heart Mr. Williams said good-by to these generous Christian natives; and then off for far-away Samoa.

Within five days he reached Savage Island, which had been so called by Captain Cook, who had this time hit the mark better than he had sometimes when naming the lands that he discovered. With a good deal of difficulty a chief was coaxed on board the ship, but perhaps Mr. Williams was sorry for his pressing invitation when he saw the behavior of his guest. He danced furiously up and down on the deck, howling frightfully, gnashing his teeth and gnawing his long beard. The worst of it was that none of his countrymen seemed any better than he, and it was no wonder that the poor teachers lost heart and begged not to be handed over to the mercy of such creatures as these. All that John Williams could do was to persuade two of the young warriors to come away with him in his ship, hoping that they might receive some good influence and after a while go back and teach their companions.

After a run of three hundred and fifty miles the Messenger of Peace reached Tonga, in the group of the Friendly Islands, where, as we shall hear by and by, the Wesleyan missionaries had already begun to work. At Tonga Mr. Williams met Fauea, a Samoan chief who had been converted in this place, and he offered to take the missionaries to his own home. The Messenger of Peace went on to Lefuga, another island of the same group, and here the missionaries came across Finau, a chief of the Vauvau Islands, where John Williams was longing to station a teacher. But Finau was not like Fauea. He was not a Christian, and had no wish that anybody else should be one. He held out little encouragement to these strangers from over the sea. He did, indeed, say that he would try to protect the life of any man who should be foolish enough to risk it among these people; but as for the people, if any of them should be converted he would at once have them put to death. The outlook was not very promising, thought John Williams, and it was hardly worth while to throw away any of his teachers under these conditions. He must lay aside his dreams for Vauvau for the present, and hope for better things in the future. His faith was to be rewarded sometime, for Savage Island and Vauvau were both in God's keeping, and were still to own him as king.

For seven days the Messenger of Peace was

tossed about in the Pacific, in the grasp of more than one violent storm; but at last the weary party sighted Savaii, the largest of the Samoan, or Navigator Islands, as they are sometimes called, perhaps, as John Williams suggested, because of the superior skill shown by the natives in building and navigating their canoes.

These islands are very beautiful, with the coral walls around them, the stretch of silver sand fringed with the foliage of the cocoanut, palm and banana trees, and the mountain slopes and the cascades beyond all touched by the peculiar yellow haze in the atmosphere. On the shore of one of these islands there is a bay called "Massacre Bay," the name coming from the fact that it was entered in 1787 by a French navigator whose crew was there brutally murdered by the natives.

In spite of their cruelty and treachery the Samoans are naturally ingenious in many ways. Their boats are made from pieces of breadfruit trees, neatly fitted one into another, and then lashed together by native twine. The houses meant for public entertainments are large, and shaped to look like something between round and oval. They are formed of two or three large posts, fixed in the ground, and a short ridge-pole, from four to six feet in length, covered with rafters and thatch. The

rafters come from the wood of the breadfruit
tree, and the leaf of the sugar-cane is used for
thatching. These buildings are usually open all
around at the sides, and are covered with mats
for carpets. The dwelling-houses are similar in
style, but lower and smaller. The Samoans had
neither temples nor altars. Their religion con-
sisted in a belief that spirits live in certain animals, and these animals were looked upon with
superstitious reverence. Sometimes a dignified
old man would be seen bowing down to a little
green lizard. They had some idea of a Supreme
Being, whom they regarded as the creator of all
things. They called him Tangaloa, and at their
great feasts, before they began to eat, some
chief would arise and say, "Thank you, great
Tangaloa, for this food." The Samoans were
the only people in Polynesia who had in their
language any word for "Thank you."

Just before Mr. Williams arived at Samoa
it had been declared by an aged chief that the
worship of spirits would soon cease in these islands, and that shortly after his own death a
great white chief would come over the water and
teach the people a new religion. The chief was
very wicked and very powerful, so that Fauea
thought with a sinking of his heart that it would
be almost impossible for the missionaries to do
anything in the face of this evil old man. But

no sooner had Fauea landed than he heard the
news of the chief's death, which so delighted him
that he began to dance about and to sing with
joy.   Then he took the copper-colored people of
his island on board the strange ship and showed
them how to receive these new friends with
courtesy and kindness.   He tried to impress
them with the idea that the white men were far
ahead of them in every respect and that they
must learn all that they could from them.   The
people were very curious about the new-comers.
They examined their dress with great care and
earnestness, and even asked Mr. Williams to pull
off his shoes so that they might see which part of
his foot was skin and which was leather.   Then
they were horrified to find that he seemed to
have no toes.   Fauea explained that these superior beings wore two kinds of covering over their
feet, and then Mr. Williams had to take off his
stockings to prove that Fauea spoke the truth.

When the king of Samoa heard that the
vessel in the harbor was what was called a
" praying ship " he sent a large quantity of
food on board and refused to take any pay for
it.   Eight men with their wives and children
then ventured to go on shore, where they were
greeted by a crowd of people bearing lighted
torches, thus forming a sort of missionary torch-
light procession.

Some remarkable customs were found in these islands also. One of them was that the women expressed their grief at the death of a friend, not by wearing black garments, but by burning themselves all over in small blisters, which they thought were very ornamental. They were fond, too, of adorning themselves with wreaths and garlands of flowers and leaves, and blue beads they admired so much that a large pig would be readily given for six of them.

The morning after the landing of the missionaries a public meeting was held at which both the king and his brother were present, although there was at that time on the island some disturbance and threatening of war following some trouble that had arisen in connection with the death of the old chief. Both men promised to take good care of the teachers that should be left with them, and before the ship sailed a giant chief from a neighboring island came over and pleaded that he might have a teacher for his people. " I will make them listen and learn," he said earnestly.

" There are two little words in our language that I have always admired," said Mr. Williams, as he set sail from Samoa. "They are 'Trust' and 'Try.'" Certainly he had reason to believe in the motto if anybody ever had, for he was al-

ways ready to act upon its advice and knew
the result of doing so.

Owing to the contrary winds he could not
stop at Savage Island on his way home, so he
pushed on to Rarotonga. The plague had disappeared, and Rarotonga was again Rarotonga,
as one man said. Then the ship called at Eimeo, where, as in the old days in Antioch, when
Paul returned from his missionary journey, the
disciples gathered to hear of the adventures
and experiences of the one who had been on a
tour among the heathen.

About this time Tamatoa, the old king of
Raiatea, died. His last words were, "Beware
lest the gospel be driven from these islands."
In 1831 John Williams again visited Rarotonga,
and from that place started on a voyage among
all the islands of the Hervey group. "The
natives cling round him, and he seems really
one with them," said the missionaries who went
with him.

On his return to Rarotonga he set to work
to finish his translation of the Bible into the
native tongue, but he was interrupted by a
fearful hurricane, which hurled down one thousand houses and helped the sea to pick up the
poor little Messenger of Peace in its arms and
wash it several miles inland, dropping it at last
in a hole five feet deep. Some of the natives

declared that the storm was the fault of the
Christians, and made that an excuse for going
back to their old ways. Others comforted themselves with the thought that the Bible was left to
them at any rate. Mr. Williams diverted their
minds by putting them to work to repair dam-
ages, but it was a month or two before the
Messenger of Peace could be dug out and again
set afloat. When once more in the water, Mr.
Williams took the boat over to Tahiti to obtain
provisions for the hungry Rarotongans, whose
crops had been destroyed.

At Raiatea Mr. Williams had to form a tem-
perance society, to withstand the evil influence
of the introduction of whiskey by a trading vessel. He carried back with him to Rarotonga
several barrels of flour, and with them as much
food as he could, buying various articles from an
American captain. He had with him, besides,
some horses, donkeys and horned cattle. These
animals amazed the natives, who had never
before seen anything like them, and they gave
them very queer names. The horse they called
"the great pig that carries the man;" the don-
key, "the noisy pig," or "the long-eared pig;"
and the dog, "the barking pig." All of these
things were of great service to the people of
Rarotonga, and so helped the missionaries in
bringing the gospel to them.

In 1832 Mr. Williams made another voyage to Samoa. On this trip, Makea, king of Raro-tonga, went with him, as well as a native convert named Teara. As they started forth on their missionary tour Teara expressed his feelings in a beautiful prayer, which it is hard to realize came from the lips of a man who nine years before had been a cannibal.

" If we fly to heaven," he said, "there, O God, we shall find thee ; if we dwell upon land, thou art there also; if we sail on the sea, thou art here. This affords us comfort, so that we sail upon the ocean without fear, because thou, O God, art in our ship. The king of our bodies has his subjects to whom he issues his orders, but if he himself goes with them his presence stimulates their zeal, they work with energy, they do it readily and they do it well. O Lord, thou art the King of our spirits ; thou hast issued orders to thy subjects to do a great work : thou hast commanded them to preach the gospel to every creature. We are going on that errand now. Let thy presence go with us to quicken us and enable us to persevere in the great work until we die. Thou hast said that thy presence shall go with thy people even to the end of the world. Fulfil, O Lord, to us this cheering promise. I see, O Lord, a compass in this ves-sel by which the seamen steer the right course

that we may escape destruction and danger. Be
to us, O Lord, like this compass, our Guide and
our Saviour."

Teara became a faithful worker and was a
great help to the missionaries, and always an
honor to the Master whom he trusted so well.

John Williams hoped that this time he might
visit every island in the Samoan group. He
stopped at several of them, and in many places
he found people who, in various ways, had caught
echoes of the gospel story from other islands
and were longing for a "religion ship" to come
along and bring them teachers for themselves.
Some of them had begun to follow in the steps
of the missionaries, and were trying, so far as
they knew how, to live the Christian life, calling
themselves "Sons of the Word."

In one spot Mr. Williams was met by a
chief who hailed him with these words: "You
need n't be afraid of us; we are Christians."

"Christians?" asked Mr. Williams. "Why,
what do you know about being Christians?"

"Why," answered the man, "there was a
great chief from the white man's country, whose
name was Williams, who came to Savaii about
twenty moons ago and placed there some workers of religion; and some of our people who
were there have come home and taught us what
he taught them."

Then he showed Mr. Williams a little chapel that had been built and told him that there were fifty persons in the congregation. The Christians were distinguished from the other natives by a piece of white cloth worn by each one around the arm.

"Well," said Mr. Williams, "I am that white man; but who preaches to the people here?"

"Oh," replied the man, "I go over to the mission station once in a while and get some religion which I bring carefully home and give to the people. Then, when that is gone, I take my canoe and go and fetch some more. Now, wont you give me a man full of religion, so that I sha'n't have to risk my life going so far to get it?"

Mr. Williams was touched by this appeal, and promised to send soon to this earnest worker some man who would be "full of religion," and be able to teach and to help these dark brothers who were striving to walk in the right way.

CHAPTER IV.

THE SAMOAN AND LOYALTY ISLANDS: THE CAPTAIN'S LAST VOYAGE.

IT was Sunday when Mr. Williams landed at the principal settlement at Savaii, and he went directly to church, where he preached to seven hundred people. It was the wildest congregation he had ever seen. Some chiefs had mats over their shoulders or tied around their waists, and their long, stiff hair stood out like the prickles of a hedgehog. Some persons had long frizzled locks, and others had their hair tied up in huge balls on the top of their heads. After the afternoon service one of the native teachers made an address, and told the people that Mr. Williams had come to prove to them that that which had been taught them was true. Then up rose the king and said, " For my part, my whole soul shall be given to the word of Jehovah, and I will use my utmost endeavors that the word of Jehovah shall encircle the land."

In the evening Mr. Williams himself preached, and this time he had about one thousand hearers. After the meeting he sat down alone and composed three hymns for the use of

the Samoans, one of which is given here, as it
reads in the translation :

> " Great is his compassion,
> His mercy to us.
> Great the love of Jesus Christ
> To die upon the earth.

> " A beloved Son was Jesus Christ,
> A very good Son ;
> But he died down here below
> To obtain salvation for us.

> " Let us every one believe
> With our whole hearts,
> That our souls may obtain salvation
> When Jesus Christ shall come."

As the king had decided to give up idolatry,
the god of war, which was only a piece of old
matting carried in the canoe of the leader in
time of war, was sentenced to be drowned. The
people felt that it would be too dreadful and dis-
graceful a death for it to be thrown into the fire
and burned. This mat was rescued by Mr. Williams, who took it to England and had it placed in
the museum of the London Missionary Society.

One great trouble that the teachers found in
trying to educate the people was the laziness of
the natives. When they had worked for five
minutes at the alphabet they would say: "Oh,
how tired we are! Let us put it away!" One
man excused himself from study by saying

grandly: "Yes, writing very good for captain;
but Samoan more clever; he can keep things in
his head; he no need writing."

This was rather discouraging, of course; but
there were some hopeful things as well.

One day Mr. Williams set out to pay a visit
to a village not far from the capital, and before
he reached the place he was met by a long procession of women each carrying a present in
her hand. The leader was a woman who had
become a Christian, and who had led nearly one
hundred other women to follow her example.
They had now formed in line to go out to
greet the man who had been the one from
whom the message had come to them through
those whom he had taught. They brought him
a baked pig, some cocoanuts, and other things
besides. They were strangely attired, in red
and white mats, and were decorated with strings
of blue beads. But John Williams was pleased
with their gratitude and their efforts to do what
they thought was right, especially as they had
no sympathy from their husbands because, as
they said sadly, "They are not yet 'Sons of the
Word.'"

Among the Samoan Islands is one that is
small and oblong, and can be reached only by
a narrow channel lying between high rocks. If
people of the neighboring island, where the

giant chief lived, are defeated in battle, they
run across to this island, throw a bridge over
the chasm, from which they can hurl stones at
the enemy, and lay a tripping-line along the
water, so that no canoe can enter the passage
without being upset.

They call themselves Malo, or Victorious,
and keep a record of their wars by dropping an
oddly shaped stone into a basket after each
victory. When Mr. Williams stopped at this
island the basket held one hundred and seven
stones. Here the Messenger of Peace was almost wrecked, but escaped uninjured.

The ship next touched at Apia, on the isl-
and of Upolu, where about eighty Christians
were found, and then called at Keppel's Island,
where a report was given of a teacher who had
influenced about five hundred natives to turn
to Christianity. Then Mr. Williams went on
to Vauvau, in the Friendly Islands, where he
learned with joy that some Wesleyan Missionaries had managed to settle, in spite of the fierce
chief Finau, and that the whole island was
Christianized.

The voyage from Vauvau to Tonga was a
rough and dangerous one. The ship sprang a
leak, and storms fell upon the passengers. But
at Tonga the trouble was remedied, and on the
fifth of December the Messenger of Peace was

off on her homeward voyage. She reached
Rarotonga after an absence of fifteen weeks.

Mr. Williams now resolved to take a little
vacation and go home, as he had been away from
England for eighteen years; so he sold his faithful little vessel, and went back to his native land.

A very warm welcome they gave him, there
in old England, and he had a great deal to tell
about his life and work down in the Pacific.
He had written an account of it all, and now
had the book published under the name of
"Missionary Enterprises in the South Seas."
Every body was eager to read it, and thirty-
six thousand copies were sold in five years.
He also raised money enough to buy a ship,
which was called the Camden, and then, not
willing to spend any more time in talking about
the past, or in enjoying the present among his
fond and admiring friends at home, his heart
began to reach out after those dark people in
the Pacific Islands, and he made ready for another voyage. On the eleventh of April, 1838,
he set forth again for the South Seas.

He went first to Samoa, and chose Upolu as
the future mission station. Then he visited
Rarotonga, and left there five thousand copies
of the New Testament and made some arrange-
ments for starting a college for the training of
native converts as teachers. He stopped too

at other islands, going at last to Raiatea, where, with the exception of two short trips to Samoa, he stayed until he went off on his final voyage.

The evening before he set out on this last journey an old blind chief came to him and begged to be taken with him.

"Teacher Williams," said the old man, "I am a blind man, but I have a great desire to go with you to the dark lands. Perhaps my being blind will make them pity me, and not kill me, and while I can talk to them, and tell them of Jesus, my boy here can read and write, and so we can teach them something."

Of course the poor old blind man could not go on the long perilous voyage, but brave tender-hearted John Williams was much touched by his devotion and earnestness, and no doubt the simple, honest, loving words came back to him with cheer and comfort during the following weeks on the stormy sea, as he sailed on towards the last harbor that he should make until he should anchor in the quiet haven of the heavenly home.

On the third of November, 1839, he preached his farewell sermon, the text of which was from Acts 20: 36–38: "And they all wept sore, and fell upon Paul's neck and kissed him, sorrowing most of all for the words which he spake, that they should see his face no more."

Did he feel, himself, the great-hearted captain, that he should never come back to these true friends of his? At any rate, he bade them good-by and sailed away for the New Hebrides, where he had long wished to scatter some gospel seed. After a run of six hundred miles the Camden made Rovuma on the twelfth of November. The next day Mr. Williams and his companions went on to the New Hebrides. On the seventeenth of November they sighted Fortuna. The natives were gathering in groups and making signs for the ship to come near. A chief, tricked out in bracelets, and with rings of tortoise-shell in his ears, came on board, and after a while a bay was found where the passengers might land. The natives seemed very friendly, but nobody could be found who would go with the Camden to Tanna. On the evening of the nineteenth the ship was lying off Erromanga. Mr. Williams said that as Samoa was now well supplied with missionaries he had thought of making his home here, but the next morning he had changed his mind and decided to go on to Aneityum, the most southerly island in the group. Still he wished to go on shore, so the small boat was lowered, and with two men, named Harris and Cunningham, he pulled away for land. They all rambled along the beach, as the natives seemed to be kindly disposed toward

them. Mr. Williams gave some of them fish-
hooks and a few small pieces of calico, and
they took them with no sign of anything but
peaceable feelings. Mr. Harris wandered on by
himself, and was lost to sight in the bush, when
suddenly there was a shriek from the savages in
that direction and Mr. Harris was seen to be
running towards the water with the natives in
hot pursuit. He was struck down by their clubs
and spears, and Mr. Cunningham called to Mr.
Williams to take flight, but he could not bear to
desert his friend, so paused a moment to see if
there were any hope of helping him. The delay
cost John Williams his life. He heard the war-
shell blown, and the war-cry sounded in his ears,
and then the savages were upon him. They
followed him into the water, where they soon
caught him and murdered him in the same way
as they had his fellow soldier. The men in the
ship were unable to lift a finger for his rescue,
but their hearts were almost broken when they
saw that he was really dead. They could hardly
believe that their leader would be among them
no more.

The grief of the people of Samoa when they
heard the sad news is almost impossible to describe. "Alas, Williams! Alas, our father!"
they cried, in sorrow and distress. A monument
was set up at Apia bearing this inscription:

"Sacred to the memory of the Rev. John Williams, father of the Samoan and other missions, aged forty-three years and five months, who was killed by the cruel natives of Erromanga, on November twentieth, 1839, while endeavoring to plant the Gospel of Peace on their shores."

But John Williams had a still better monument in the work that had been accomplished among the islands that he loved so well. When he died there were in Raiatea, in place of the old huts and poor little villages, English-looking cottages, each one with its own garden; and instead of wild, ignorant savages there were well-dressed children, with book and slate in hand, going back and forth from school. On Sundays there were many people on their way to church, with their Bibles and their hymn-books tied up in their handkerchiefs, in South Sea Island fashion, and there were few households in which family worship was not a regular part of the opening and the closing of each day. It is much the same with the other islands of the group.

Then there was Rarotonga. In two years heathenism had been swept off the island. One old man of this place used to say that he had lived through the reign of four kings. "During the first," he said, "we were always at war.

During the second, we were almost destroyed by a great famine. During the third, we were the prey of two other settlements. But during this reign we were visited by another King; a good King; a powerful King; a King of love: Jesus, the Lord from heaven. He has gained the victory. He has conquered our hearts. We are all his subjects. Therefore we now have peace and plenty in this world, and hope soon to dwell with him in heaven."

The natives of Rarotonga have carried the gospel to the Loyalty Islands, to New Caledonia and to New Guinea. These native teachers have far more influence with the people than have the white men. They are simple and earnest, and their hearts are all in the work. They have been trained as warriors, and they know how to obey and to give their minds to what they are doing.

"We are now the soldiers of Jesus Christ," they say, "tell us what he would like us to do." If they are told that their Master would not wish them to go to a certain place, they answer at once, "Then we wont go;" or if some one says, "He would be sorry to hear you use such language," they reply, "Then we wont say that any more;" or if it is hinted that he would rather not have them do a certain thing, they still respond, "Then we wont do it." No wonder that

they can win a hearing from others when they
learn so well their own lessons.

One of the converts of Rarotonga longed to
work for others just as his teacher, John Williams, had worked; so in the ship named after
the good captain this man Pao went to Mari,
an island about fifty miles from Lifu, in the Loyalty group. He was to stay and study with
the missionaries who were stationed there and
then go on to Lifu. But Pao learned the language as quickly as he could, and then, persuad-
ing a native of Mari to accompany him, he set
out in a canoe for Lifu, feeling that he could
wait no longer. He was received in a friendly
manner by the natives, in spite of the fact that
they were all cannibals. The medicine men, it
is true, did not like him very well; they feared
that he would interfere with their business; but
he did succeed in interesting most of the people,
and even made friends with their enemies on
the opposite side of the island. In course of
time whole villages burned their idols and
placed themselves under Christian teaching, and
in twelve years the whole population of about
ten thousand had accepted the gospel. The
language was reduced to writing, and a school-
book, catechism, hymn-book, and the New Testament and Psalms were translated into the native tongue, for by this time other missionaries

had come over to help. Schools and churches were built in almost every village, and were filled with those who were eager to hear and to learn. A seminary had been started for the education of native pastors and teachers, and a missionary society had been formed that had sent workers to New Caledonia and the New Hebrides. The natives had good houses, fine roads, and many of the conveniences and comforts of civilized life. Several European shops had been opened, and traders often visited the island.

The French have also interfered with work in the Loyalty Islands. The French governor of Lifu asked one of the native teachers, " Who told you to come here ?" " My Master said to me, ' Go ye into all the world to preach the gospel.' That is what brought me here," replied the man. This reply was thought impudent, and the teacher was imprisoned for three days and then sent away. In Mari, a missionary who had labored there for thirty-four years was obliged to leave his charge, and the French government does all in its power to defeat the aims of the Protestants. Still the converts are true to their teaching.

As for the church at Samoa, it has always been overflowing with missionary spirit. Those people have taken the gospel to the Tokelan and Ellice Islands and to the Gilbert Islands, south of the Equator, and under the direction of their missionaries, Mr. A. Murray and Mr. George Turner, they began work in the New Hebrides. That dreadful Savage Island, too, where John Williams dared not land, has been completely Christianized through their efforts.

It was in 1861 that a party set out for the Ellice group, but the frail vessel being over-taken by a storm was driven about by winds and currents for eight weeks. At the end of that time the crew stumbled upon one of the Ellice Islands, where they found that the people had gained a little religious knowledge from the sailors of a trading-vessel and had burned their idols. They were so hungry for the Bible that one of the new comers had to tear apart his Rarotongan New Testament, and give it out in bits to the natives.

From this spot the gospel was carried to other islands. In one place the people had ob-tained a copy of the English Bible, which they kept wrapped in a large cotton handkerchief during the week, but which on Sunday was brought out and laid open in sight of the natives, who gathered round it and sang songs taught them by some visitors.

The Samoans now have the whole Bible in their own tongue, a school for native teachers and preachers, and besides having built their

own churches and pastors' houses they have
sent $6.500 every year to the London Mission-
ary Society to help carry on its work.   In 1892
they gave $9,000 as a thank offering for having
the gospel themselves.   They have a beautiful
custom in their churches of keeping on their
books the names of members who have died,
with a mark following each one which means
that they will not think of that one as dead
either to them or to the cause, and a contribtion
will always be made for him by his friends.

The Christian population is thirty-six thousand, among fifty thousand inhabitants.   In
the largest of the islands there are not fifty families where morning and evening worship is not
a daily custom.   There is a great demand for
the pocket edition of the Bible.   A large number were sold in a short time, and there was a
call for five thousand more.

The king of Samoa has recently issued an
order that no intoxicating drink whatever shall
be given, sold, or offered to be bought or bartered
by any native Samoan, or any Pacific Islander
resident in Samoa.

Robert Louis Stevenson, the distinguished
writer, who lived for a long time in Samoa, said
that when he went there he was much prejudiced
against missions, but after having seen them on
their own ground his objections vanished, and

he felt instead a great regard and admiration for the work. He advises anybody who has any ideas like those he once held to try the same cure and study missions on the spot.

And so John Williams lived long enough to be able to say that there was no island within two thousand miles of Tahiti that had not heard the gospel story, and when he fell by the hand of the savages the work was taken up and carried on by others who were led by his example or who had been trained by him. What that old missionary, Paul, said about himself would, with a little change of name, be true of John Williams: "I have planted, Apollos watered, but God gave the increase." 1 Cor. 3:6.

When the Bishop of Ripon laid down the story of John Williams' life he said, "I have now been reading the twenty-ninth chapter of the Acts of the Apostles."

CHAPTER V.

NEW ZEALAND AND THE FRIENDLY ISLANDS : ISL-ANDS UNWORTHY OF THEIR NAME.

BEFORE going on to the Friendly Islands to take up the work there with the Wesleyan missionaries, of whom we have already had a glimpse or two, we must stop at big New Zea-land, and see what is going on at that place.

New Zealand is really made up of two large islands and several smaller ones. The whole group is nearly one thousand miles long and two hundred miles broad. The cluster was first found by the Dutch navigator, Tasman, in 1642, and was afterward visited by Capt. Cook, in 1769.

The inhabitants were called Maoris, and they are supposed to have come originally from the Samoan Islands. The men were usually about five feet, six inches high, and weighed about one hundred and forty pounds. The hair of the New Zealanders was generally coarse and black, although sometimes it was a rusty red. Their eyes were dark brown, and their skin was olive-brown, in some cases almost black. They were savages and cannibals, like so many of their

neighbors, tattooing themselves by way of adorn-
ment, and killing one another by way of pastime.   They used to thrust pebbles down the
throats of their children, in order, as they hoped,
to make their hearts hard and pitiless.

They were very superstitious, and when they
were ill they believed that their god came to
them in the form of a lizard, and, entering the
side, gnawed at the organs that were necessary
to life.   When a person had a pain in his back
he would lie down and ask another man to jump
over him and then stamp upon him to press out
the pain.

Their houses were built of bulrushes, and
were lined with the leaves of the palm-tree
neatly braided together.   They were about four
or five feet high.   The people had no furniture,
and their cooking utensils were a few stones.
They had an idea that there was a great Being
somewhere who sent the thunder, but they were
much afraid of him and had no form of worship.   They had some notion of a future life, but
they thought that it would be much like this
one ; and on the death of a chief his slaves were
killed, that they might go with him and wait
upon him.   Altogether it did not seem an invi-
ting spot for missionaries to settle in, but the
need was great and some men were raised up to
throw their lives into this great field.

QUEEN POMARE'S TOMB, TAHITI.

The first missionary to the country was Samuel Marsden, a British chaplain in New South Wales. In 1814 he began a mission on the eastern coast of the northern island. The islanders were known to be so savage that no ship captain would take him to the shore, so he had to buy a brig at his own expense and landed with a single companion.

Just about this time there was a young man in England, named Nathaniel Turner, who was a member of the Wesleyan Methodist Church. He thought that he heard a voice, deep down in his heart, saying to him, "Go carry the glad tidings to the heathen! Go carry the glad tidings to the heathen!" He listened to the command, and offered himself to the church as a missionary, but the church was in debt, and there was no money with which to send the young soldier out to fight for his Master. He must wait, he was told, until the necessary sum could be raised.

But there was another side to the story. Soon afterwards a Mr. Leigh, who had been a missionary in New South Wales, and who had gone to New Zealand for the benefit of his health, came home to England for a little rest and change. His heart was full of the sad condition of the people of New Zealand and he could not keep from talking about it wherever he

went. He begged the society to let him have
a missionary for New Zealand; and when he
heard that there was a young man only waiting
for a fund to be raised for his support before
setting out to a foreign land he made up his
mind that the lacking means should be supplied.
After asking permission he started out to collect
articles of manufacture that would be as useful
as money to the missionaries, as they could barter
them among the natives for food, land and building material, and he succeeded in gathering a
large number of axes, razors, fish-hooks, pots,
kettles, prints, and calicoes. When he thought
that he had enough of this kind of currency he
sent off a message to Nathaniel Turner, " Prepare to go to New Zealand at once."

This was short notice, but Mr. Turner was
quite ready for marching orders at any moment.
There was a brave girl in England who had
promised to go with him wherever he should
be sent, and now she must be married to him in
haste and fly away with him on the long wed-
ding journey across the seas. On the third of
August, 1823, in the year that John Williams
found Rarotonga, Nathaniel Turner and his
little bride landed at the Bay of Islands, from
which place they were taken forty miles inland
to the spot that had been chosen by Mr. Leigh
for the mission station.

Mr. Leigh was there before them, but they found him ill from the effects of the climate. The mission house, which was not yet completed, stood in a lovely quiet valley, surrounded by mountains and with a river rippling through it down to the sea, but the rainy season had begun and the roof of the new building was not water-proof. Mr. Leigh had been sleeping in an empty cask, in order to keep himself dry.

Soon he had to go away and leave the two young people to look after themselves. But they did not lose heart. They had three assistant workers, and finding a better building site they set up a frame cottage that they had brought from Sydney.

The chief of the region, whose civilized name was George, pretended at first to have most kindly intentions towards the strangers who had come to live with him, but no sooner was the little home ready for use than up stepped the big chief and said coolly, " This house is mine ; I will knock it down. You shall go away." The natives with him made a dash at the workmen and seized their spades, and then began a horrible howling, which they kept up both night and day for a long time. This kind of serenade did not make the new abode very cheerful, but fortunately the throats of the savages could not stand this exercise forever, and fresh ways of tormenting the teachers had to be invented.

The chief wished to be paid several times over for every article that he exchanged with the missionaries, and when he could not have his own will in the matter he threatened to shoot Mr. Turner. "You want to make us slaves," he said angrily. "We want muskets, powder, and tomahawks. You give us nothing but prayers. We don't want to hear about Jesus Christ. If you love us, as you say you do, give us blankets."

He also said that he meant to kill Mrs. Turner and her maid, but after a while his rage died out, and he seemed sorry for his bursts of passion.

"When my heart rests here," he said, laying his hand upon his breast, "then I love Mr. Turner very much; but when my heart rises to my throat, then I could kill him in a moment."

One cannot altogether blame those poor natives for their enmity to the white people. They had been so often ill-treated and deceived by the traders that it is not strange that they were a little suspicious and bitter in their feelings towards every pale-face. The missionaries realized that they were dealing with ignorant, quick-tempered savages, and kept tight hold of their patience, faith and love, in spite of many sad discouragements. They studied the languages, taught the children, and within a year built two chapels with their own hands. The natives continued to steal their goods, and still tried to take their lives, but after all they did learn to respect these friends, so brave and kind and forbearing. "We have tried all we could to make them afraid," the men owned to a visitor from another island, "but we can't do it. They are a courageous tribe."

Feeling the power of their devotion and heroism, the people began to come to church in large numbers, and listened quietly to what was said. They also sent their children to school. But this happy state of things did not last long. A whaling boat was captured by the islanders, and most of the crew murdered. This deed seemed to rouse all the old wicked, angry feelings of the natives. They were afraid, too, that England would send somebody down to punish them for their evil deed, and there was prospect of war with another island, just then, besides. In their fear and rage and excitement they fell upon the persons nearest at hand, and the missionaries saw that there was no hope of doing anything with them in their present state of mind, and thought that perhaps they would better withdraw from the scene for a while.

But they had to leave much more suddenly than they had expected. One night in January, in the year 1827, the station was attacked, and the men and women had to flee for their lives. Mrs. Turner had a narrow escape from death, for one of the savages had raised his spear to strike her down when a friendly native pushed up a shelf over the doorway and caused a large number of nails that were lying there to come tumbling and rattling down upon the head of the pursuer, which frightened him so much that he dropped his arm and gave up the chase.

Over the fields they went, the homeless little band! There were three missionaries and three children, one of the latter a baby only four weeks old. Four times they had to wade the winding river, and twice they were met by war parties, but they passed on uninjured. After a long walk of twenty miles they reached the station of the Church Missionary Society.

They had but one convert to show for all their work, but Mrs. Turner gave no signs of wishing to desert the cause yet. "Can't we stay and carry on our mission somewhere else?" she said. But this plan seemed out of the question for the present, so, after spending six months in Sydney, in Australia, the outcasts from one field resolved to take up work in another. In company with some other missionaries they went to the help of the Tonga mission, in the Friendly Islands.

The Friendly Islands also had been discovered by Capt. Cook, but he had made a slight mistake in giving this group its name. Closer acquaintance had made clear the fact that the English language could hardly have furnished a more unsuitable adjective with which to describe the inhabitants. The first missionaries, who had gone to the islands in 1796, had had to leave the place on account of most unfriendly treatment, and the second set were about to follow their example when the new force of workers lent them an extra spark of courage and hope, and made them willing to wait a while longer and try again.

The houses of Tonga were thatched with reeds of sugar-cane, and the walls were of plaited cocoa-palm leaves. They had no stone foundations to raise them above the damp earth, and in many of the poorer huts the floors were merely strewn with dried grass.

There was usually an inner room screened off for a sleeping room. The pillow was a bit of bamboo supported by two legs. The people are strong and robust, and have bright complexions. They are more intelligent than many of their neighbors, and have a good deal of influence over surrounding islands. They seemed to have more noble traits than many of the South Sea Islanders, although they were very ignorant, and had no religious knowledge. They had never heard of fire, and ate everything raw, and they had no idea that water could be made to boil. They were almost ready to worship as a god anybody who could bring to pass anything so wonderful ; and one man who thrust his hand into a kettle of hot water drew it quickly out again, saying ruefully, " The water has bitten my hand."

In 1826 a good missionary named John Thomas had gone to Tonga, and now he and his company and the new band worked on together. There were still many hardships and trials to endure before there was much encouragement. Then there was a little breath of life, like a faint ripple of wind that steals over the water and whispers hope to a becalmed vessel. King George of Haabai, an island in the Friendly group, came across to Tonga for a visit. He was a fierce, warlike savage, devoted to his idols and his strange, heathen superstitions ; but he was deeply interested and really impressed by what he heard from the teachers in Tonga, and when he went home he took down his idols from their position of honor, and, to the horror and alarm of his people, hung them in a row from his ceiling, leaving them dangling there, to show how helpless and worthless they were.

Next he built a church and asked that a missionary might be sent over to preach in it, but as there was then no missionary to spare he persuaded an English sailor who was living in Haabai to read the church service to the congregation every Sunday.

A remarkable story is told in connection with the settling of a missionary in this island. Over in Tonga, John Thomas was wondering if it would be advisable to go to the extra expense of establishing a mission on Haabai; and while he was praying and thinking over the question there was washed ashore one day an old cask in which was found a letter containing instructions about this very matter, and promising support in carrying out the plan that the missionaries had in mind. The ship bearing the letter had been wrecked, and the captain had set the message adrift, trusting that it might reach its destination. In 1830, therefore, John Thomas went to Haabai and there he preached to the natives, and after a few months several of them were baptized.

King George then paid a visit to Vauvau, where lived the surly chief Finau, who had not shown himself very cordial in his reception of John Williams' proposition to send him teachers. But King George made him listen to what he had to tell and tried to coax him into giving up his idols. After a while Finau consented to find out by an experiment the truth of what was said. He built a huge bonfire and then brought out his gods and placed them before it. "Now," said he, "if you are good for anything you can save yourselves by running away." Then he took the idols, one by one, into his hands, and holding them over the fire said to each in turn, "Run, or be burned! Run, or be burned!" As not a single image made a motion to leave the spot, he flung them all into the flames, with a scornful laugh, and believed in them no longer.

Vauvau is a dreary, lonely sort of a place. The people are shut in by tall crags; there is little growth of any kind on the island, and the only sound that can be heard is the moaning of the sea as it rushes in under the rocks. But hearing of the interest in this place Mr. and Mrs. Turner decided to go down to see if they could do anything to help at this time. One of the first things that they did was to begin to pray earnestly for all the people of the Friendly Islands, and the good Father above listened to the petitions of his servants on the desolate little island and sent them a rich blessing.

In 1834 a wonderful revival began in Vauvau. King George heard of the great awakening that

had come to his neighbors and went over to see
what was taking place, and there he was converted and took the first steps in a Christian life
that proved to be one of the most earnest that
has ever been lived. He became a local preacher, and was very helpful in carrying the gospel to
others. The good work spread from Vauvau to
Haabai and Tonga and through all the islands
of the group. In Vauvau for a week or two the
schools had to be closed and prayer-meetings
were held five or six times a day. About one
thousand persons were converted in a day. In
the other islands there were at least two thousand conversions in the course of two weeks.

King George built a large chapel in Haabai
for the use of the missionaries. It was big
enough to hold all the people of the island.
Every one of the natives wished to do something to help in the building, and the work was
regularly divided among the inhabitants of the
group. As they had no nails the timbers had to
be fastened with cords made from the fibres
of the cocoanut husks, dyed black, red, and other
colors, and beautifully woven together in artistic
patterns. The king gave to his new sanctuary
several finely-carved spears, that had been left to
him by his ancestors and had often been used
in war. They were made into rails for the com-
munion table ; and two handsome clubs, which

had been worshipped as gods, were placed at the bottom of the pulpit stairs.

So it was that when John Williams stopped at Vauvau, on his way home from Samoa, he found that the whole island had become Christian, as was said before.

Next a printing-press was set up in Tonga, and the people became much interested in the books that were printed. A great many persons began to come to the schools and converts began to start out to preach the gospel to other islands.

When Finau died King George became ruler of all the islands, and a good ruler he was indeed. He was six feet four inches in height, well-formed and athletic, and had a most intelligent, trustworthy face, with the bearing and manners of a true gentleman. He was an unmistakable Christian king. His kingdom had, in course of time, a constitution, with all the laws and regulations needed in a civilized nation. The people of the Friendly Islands are now amiable and courteous, and the women are kindly treated. Their homes are pleasant and their grounds are laid out with taste and care. For some years they have supplied fine native teachers and preachers and have sent out many missionaries, giving large sums to the Wesleyan Missionary Society—even so much as $15,000 in a year.

There are now about thirty thousand church-members in these islands. When a collection is taken in any of the churches it is said that there is never a penny, nor copper in any form, put into the plate. Nothing but gold or silver is offered to the Lord's work. On one occasion King George and his wife dropped in ten sovereigns, a gift to them from the captain of an English war-ship.

Several years ago the commander of one of these English war-ships, who had been cruising about in the Southern Pacific, stopped at the Friendly Islands. When King George came out to meet him in his royal canoe, and wearing the dress of a British officer, the commander exclaimed ; " He is every inch a king. Give him twenty-one guns !"—a royal salute.

About twenty men from Tonga were recently beaten and driven away from their homes by the remnants of the heathen party in the island. The governor of Fiji became interested in them and obtained liberty for them to return. As they sailed away from Fiji, singing, " Home, Sweet Home," the governor turned to a friend standing near by and said, " That is as fine a group of Christian gentlemen as I ever saw."

And so at last the Friendly Islands have begun to live up to their name.

CHAPTER VI.

NEW ZEALAND AND THE MELANESIAN MISSION.
TWO COLLEGE ATHLETES.

BEFORE all these great things were accomplished Mr. Turner went back to New Zealand. Other missionaries had been there in the meantime, and a change had come over the people. But all the difficulties had not yet been removed, and there were still many foes to face and many battles to be won. The old warlike spirit would break out once in a while even among those who had been studying the gospel of peace, but Mr. Turner came in with new help and inspiration, and the churches grew, and the converts became more earnest. Mr. Turner worked in New Zealand until his health failed and he had to give up his position. The rest of his life he spent in Sydney, in Australia, and he died in 1864.

In 1841 George Augustus Selwyn, of the English church, was made a missionary bishop and sent to New Zealand to look after the ministers and teachers already there under the care of the Church Missionary Society. He was a young man, about thirty-three years old, strong, bright, and athletic, and with a highly cultivated mind. He had been a famous oarsman at Cambridge, and he could manage a schooner at sea like an old sailor. Now he threw all his unusual gifts and graces and accomplishments into the work before him. He went over all the island on foot, and became acquainted with almost every nook and corner of it. In 1849 he obtained a small schooner, which went by the name of Undine, and started off on a tour of inspection.

He sailed one thousand miles, to Aneityum, in the New Hebrides, where John Geddie had just gone to work among his special group of cannibals, and taking Mr. Geddie with him he visited all the islands in the New Hebrides and Loyalty groups, and in the cluster called New Caledonia. Selwyn had marvellous art in winning the confidence of the savages. He would go among them altogether unarmed, only keeping his eye on them to make sure that they meant no mischief. Everywhere he went he would pick up a few words from the natives, and jot them down in his note-book, with the names of chiefs and of places, and then when he came again he would surprise and delight his new friends by using their language, and by seeming to know all about them. Each year he ventured a little farther on his voyages, until at last he had called at most of the islands between New

Zealand and the Solomon group. He was equal
to almost everything that came in his way, from
drawing charts and pulling ropes to making
frocks for the women and taking care of poor
sick little babies.

In 1850 an Australasian Board of Missions
was established and New Zealand fell under the
care of this Board.   In 1851 the Bishop of New-
castle in New South Wales, who had been an
old comrade of Selwyn's on the Cambridge University boat crew, went off with Selwyn on a
voyage.

Bishop Selwyn was anxious to take a few
boys to Auckland, teach them something about
Christianity, and then send them home to tell to
their friends what they had learned.

He was able to buy a larger boat, and in 1852
he carried a missionary and his wife to Aneityum free of expense. This was the beginning
of what is called the Melanesian Mission—Melanesian meaning the " Black Islands."

In 1852 also Bishop Selwyn returned to
England to tell about the work in Melanesia
and to interest others in those distant lands.
He made a deep impression, with his stirring
sermons, and among other hearts that were
especially roused was that of young John Coleridge Patteson.

"Coley" Patteson, as he was called, had begun life with many advantages. He had a strong, true man for a father, and a gentle, wise and lovely woman for a mother, and his home was of just the kind to make a brave, manly, honest boy, both high-spirited and affectionate, winning and commanding. He was very fond of reading, and after his fifth birthday, when he received a present of a Bible, he became a great student of that book.

There were some questions that his bright little brain had to struggle over; one was, "What became of the fishes during the flood?" and one day when his companions in the nursery called him impatiently to come and join in their play he said, absently, "Please wait a few minutes, while I finish the binding of Satan for a thousand years." This same little Bible that he loved so dearly when he was a boy was used, twenty-seven years later, when Coleridge Patteson was consecrated to the office of a bishop.

Early in life he began to plan for the future. At one time he heard the story of a missionary bishop who had in his field of labor undergone the experience of a terrible hurricane. "When I grow up," said small John to his mother, "I am going to be a bishop and have a hurricane too."

In course of time he went to school, after the fashion of most boys, and in the old Foundation

School at Ottery St. Mary, he studied his lessons, wrote home-sick letters to his mother, and enjoyed himself, in spite of an occasional longing look in another direction. He loved football and cricket, and would settle down to his books in good earnest so that he might push them out of the way and be free for out-of-door sports. He was only eight years old when first sent to this school, but he stood up for himself among the elder boys and took care of his younger brother as well.

Once he broke his collar-bone, but nobody knew anything about it until three weeks afterwards, when he went home and his mother saw that something hurt him when she gave him a motherly hug in greeting. When she told him that he had done wrong not to make known his accident, he said simply, " Oh, well, I did n't want to make a fuss."

When he went to Eton he was the same sort of a boy. He was always a leader, always full of life, energy and fun, but always staunch, straightforward and noble.

One Sunday afternoon he heard Bishop Selwyn speak in the parish church of New Windsor. Young Patteson stood in the aisle, as there was no seat for him, and in his white collar and short jacket, with his fair hair and earnest blue eyes, he looked like a little knight hearing the

bugle-call to battle as he listened, wholly ab-
sorbed, to the ringing words of the bishop.

The text was, "Thy heart shall be enlarged
because the abundance of the sea shall be converted unto thee, the forces also of the Gentiles
shall come unto thee."

After the meeting Coleridge ran home and
sat down and scribbled a letter to his mother
to tell her all about it.

"It was beautiful," he wrote.   "When he
talked of his going out to found a church, and
then to die neglected and forgotten, all the
people burst out crying, he was so very much
beloved by his parishioners.   He spoke of his
perils, and putting his trust in God, and then,
when he had finished, I think I never heard
anything like the sensation—a kind of feeling
that, if it had not been on so sacred a spot, all
would have exclaimed, 'God bless him!'"

Before Bishop Selwyn left England he called
upon the Pattesons to say good-by.   As he was
about to depart he said gently, "Lady Patteson,
will you give me Coley?"   This was a hard question, but the answer of the mother was given
to her boy when he came to her with the same
thought, and she promised him that if he kept
the desire as he grew older she would let him
join the bishop in his work.

But it was Coleridge who had to give up his

mother before the time came when she could give up her son. His first great trial was the death of this mother whom he loved so well. He was almost broken-hearted over his loss, but he went back to school all the purer and better for this shadow over his life. He was as athletic and as popular as ever, and in one of the annual cricket contests with Harrow he broke the powerful bowling of the other side and by putting on fifty runs to the score won the match, to his own glory and the joy of his fellow students.

His popularity and sociability brought peculiar temptations to him, but he saw things with clearer eyes than most of his companions and he came through unhurt. On an occasion of a dinner of the Eton eleven certain objectionable songs were started. Coleridge, who was chairman at the time, tried to hush them up, but one boy persisted in going on with his occupation. Coleridge at once arose and said calmly, " If this does n't stop I shall leave the room." And leave the room he did, and the next day sent in his resignation as captain ; nor would he take up the position again until his schoolfellows came and apologized to him, and promised that nothing of the sort should happen again as long as the present eleven stayed in the school.

TARAVAO BAY, TAHITI.

From Eton he stepped into University life at Oxford, where he became a great student. He chose the ministry for his occupation, and in course of time was happily settled in England, at Alfington, in Devonshire; but in the year 1854 came his second call to work for God in foreign lands. When Bishop Selwyn again returned to England all the old admiration and enthusiasm once awakened by his presence flamed up again in Coleridge Patteson's heart. In a conversation with the bishop he showed that his early purpose was still in his mind, but the thought of his father kept him in England. The bishop pointed out to him that if he meant to devote his life to missionary labor he should begin while he was strong and vigorous, and the result was that the father was asked if he could let his son go to New Zealand, "Oh I can't let him go," cried the old judge at first, but immediately added, with that generosity and courage that his son had inherited from him, "God forbid that I should stop him !"

So, difficult as was the task, Coleridge Patteson turned his back upon his family and home, and the brilliant prospects opening before him, and trying to forget himself, and to think only of his work, he followed the good bishop over the sea.

On the voyage the young missionary studied

the language of New Zealand and learned a
good deal about navigation. When he reached
Auckland he set to work to master his new
duties. He was placed in the college, where
among other things he had to make his own
bed, keep his room in order, and clear away
things after meals. He was very quick in ac-
quiring the language, and the natives used
to say to him, "We want you. You speak so
plainly we can understand you." They were
pleased, too, with his readiness to do anything
that came in his way, from writing a sermon
to cooking a dinner. "Gentleman-gentleman
thought nothing that ought to be done too
mean for him; pig-gentleman never work," they
said approvingly, in the words of one of their
proverbs.

In the Southern Cross he went off with the
bishop on his missionary cruises among the
islands of Melanesia. They had many narrow
escapes in their visits to the islanders, and saw
some strange sights, but Patteson looked below the surface and found much that was good
and attractive in these children of the sea.
"They are fond; that is the name for them,"
he wrote home. "I have had boys and men,
in a few minutes after landing, follow me like
a dog, holding their hands in mine as a little
child does with its nurse." He never called

them savages, but spoke of them as " my Melanesians."

There was probably something in Patteson
himself that invited this confidence. Often
when a native had lifted his arm to send an
arrow flying at the strangers stepping upon the
beach, he would look up, with his warm, bright
smile, and the arrow would fall harmlessly to
the ground. The boys that he taught and knew
and loved he addressed by a name that meant
" old fellow."

When he settled down with his pupils at
St. John's College, in Auckland, he was to them
a father, a friend, a playmate, all in one. He
taught them cricket, and printing, and weaving,
besides those things that they learned from
books, and when they were sick he gave up
his own bed to them and nursed them with
care and tenderness. That they were making
progress, too, in the highest education was
proved by their prayers.

One boy of seventeen prayed in this way:
"O God, thou strengthenest us. Thou lovest
us. We have come from a distant land and
no evil has happened to us, for thou lovest us.
Thou hast provided us with a missionary to
live here with us. Give us strength from thee
every day. We are men who have done evil
before thee, but thou watchest over us, and

savest us from the hands of Satan. We do not wish to follow him, but to be thy servants, O Jesus, and the servants of thy great Father, and of the Holy Spirit who giveth us life for evermore."

CHAPTER VII.

THE MELANESIAN MISSION: THE BISHOP AND HIS BOYS.

SOME of the boys who were gathered for training in the college at Auckland were so delicate in health that it seemed best to start a school in some island that would be sufficiently sheltered for a winter residence. Lifu was the island chosen, and in this spot Patteson stayed for three weeks, teaching a class of twenty-five young men. The only comment that he made upon his life in this place was, "Of course I should have been glad sometimes for a good talk in English with somebody."

The college was moved from Auckland to another site, about two miles away. Here he had a class of small boys; "the jolliest little fellows," he wrote, "seven of them, and scarcely too big to take on my knee and talk to about God and heaven and Jesus Christ."

About this time Patteson made a cruise in an open boat to Saddle Island, but met with much stormy weather, and the hardships and exposure of this voyage caused on his return a painful tumor in his ear. Sometimes he would walk up

and down all night in agony ; but this affliction
he bore with his usual fortitude and patience.

In 1861 John Coleridge Patteson was consecrated missionary bishop of Melanesia. When
the news reached England the aged father
prayed at family prayers more earnestly than
usual for all missionaries, adding in a trembling
voice, "especially for John Coleridge Patteson,
missionary bishop."

Not long afterwards the good old man was
called home to the Father's house, and under
this fresh sorrow Patteson's health for a while
gave way, and he left his work to go off on a
cruise among the islands.

Then he returned to his pupils, who clustered
round him, as somebody said, "like chickens
round a hen."   When he came out of his rooms
towards evening, when the boys were playing
on the beach, there would be an immediate rush
at him.   Some of the youngsters would lay hold
of his hands, some would seize the skirts of his
coat, and each one had some special word for
him.   He would throw his arms round the neck
of one of the taller boys, and with the rest
clinging to him in one way or another they
would stroll off together for a walk.

The bishop still continued his voyages,
preaching to the people on the islands, collect-
ing boys for the schools and trying to do some-

thing against the stealing of the natives by the slave-dealers from Queensland and other colonies. The slave-ships were called by the people the "snatch-snatch boats," or "kill-kill vessels." The traders used very mean methods for the purpose of luring the natives to their ships, often telling them that the bishop was on board and wished to see some of them, and then making off with those who were simple enough to put themselves in their power.

Patteson said that he found that two of the first words learned by islanders were "tobacco" and "missionary." The former word was taught them by the men who carried on the dreadful traffic in human beings and also planted in their minds seeds of distrust and hatred towards all of the white race.

The bishop himself was often in danger. At one time when landing upon an island he saw by the gestures of the men that they meant to kill him. He asked permission to rest for a moment in a hut by the wayside, and there he fell upon his knees and prayed earnestly that if his last hour had come help might still be sent to these poor people. When he rose there was a look on his face that so overawed the savages that they gave up their evil purpose and took him in safety back to his boat.

The boat called the Southern Cross, which

Selwyn and Patteson had brought with them from England, had been wrecked on some rocks known as the "Hen and Chickens," but a second boat of the name was sent to Bishop Patteson from home, and became of great service to him.

He next paid a visit to Australia, where he engaged so much interest in his mission that he raised a large sum of money for his work.

During his following voyage he landed at Santa Cruz. All went well until he returned to his boat, when the natives sent a shower of arrows flying after him. The bishop was unhurt, but two of his dear native Christian boys were killed. The last words of one of them were, "They never stop singing there, sir, do they?" and so he passed away to the heavenly home of which he was thinking. This was a severe trial to the bishop but did not make him stop work. He gained a good deal of strength and consolation from a book sent him by his sister, the copy of the "Imitation of Christ" that had belonged to brave young Bishop Mackenzie, who had laid down his life in Africa. The headquarters of the mission were removed to Norfolk Island, and soon afterwards Bishop Selwyn went back to England.

It was hard for the two men to part. There were a few choked words; each tried to say, "God bless you," and that was all: but in a let-

ter home Patteson said sadly, " I feel as though
my master had been taken from my head."

A great joy came to him, however, when one
of his native deacons was ordained as the first
Melanesian Christian minister.

There were by this time many English colonists settled in New Zealand, and sometimes
the new-comers would help themselves unfair-
ly to the lands of the natives, which caused
trouble and led to wars. Some of the people of
New Zealand, as they learned to hate the British residents, began to dislike their religion as
well, and so they invented one of their own,
called Howism ; those who took it up going by
the name of How Hows, the title being derived
from the sound of their war-cry, which resem-
bles the barking of a dog. This religion was a
mixture of truths from the Bible and old superstitions of their own, and the movement was really a return to heathenism. But in all the
anger and excitement of these people they still
showed traces of nobility and a remembrance
and appreciation of the Christian ideas that had
been taught them. They would allow wagons
loaded with provisions and ammunition to pass
them untouched on Sunday, and they took care
of the wounded and allowed the dead to be buried. In one battle the commander wrote on the
orders of the day, " If thine enemy hunger, feed

him ; if he thirst, give him drink ;" and then, after the fight, he crept through the English lines at the risk of his own life to carry a cup of water to a wounded enemy who lay dying within the pales.

About 1872 the warfare was given up and matters between the natives and the colonists have been going on more quietly.

Bishop Patteson went on with his voyages until his mission had spread as far as the Solomon and Banks Islands; but at last he lost his life in the cause to which he was devoting himself, and by means of the people he was trying to save.

The slave-traders, wishing to entrap more of the natives for their wicked designs, had gone farther than ever in their wiles. At one time one of them arrayed himself in a dress like the bishop's and held a mock service on board the ship, in order to entice the people whom they were seeking to come out to them. The plan was successful, and a large number of slaves was captured. This deed roused the hatred and suspicion of the deceived natives, and Bishop Patteson was the victim of their revenge. He had started on a trip to the Santa Cruz group of islands, and on September twentieth, 1871, the Southern Cross was headed towards Nukapu. The bishop was talking to the young Melanesians who were with him, and his closing words were these : " And I say unto you, my friends, be not afraid of them that kill the body, and after that have no more that they can do."

They drew near the island, and the bishop went ashore. No sooner had he landed than the men in the canoes along the coast drew their bows and began to fire upon their boat. The crew became anxious about the bishop and some of them set out to look for him, but before they had gone far a canoe was sent floating out from the beach to meet them. As it approached they saw with beating hearts that it held the dead body of a man. It was that of their be-loved bishop. A peaceful smile was on his face, but it was found that he had been wounded in five places. The fact that each wound had been given to avenge some native death was signified by a palm-leaf tied in five knots and laid upon his breast. As his sad-hearted comrades looked down at his sleeping form did they not think of the words of Coleridge Patteson's Master, " Greater love hath no man than this—that a man lay down his life for his friends"?

On this little island now stands an iron cross, twelve feet high, bearing this inscription :

"In Memory of

JOHN COLERIDGE PATTESON, D. D.,

Missionary Bishop,

Whose life was here taken by men for whom he
would gladly have given it."

Other memorials were erected in England;
one is at Sperne Cross, near Exeter, and one is
the magnificent pulpit in Exeter Cathedral.

Bishop Patteson left his whole fortune of
$65,000 to the mission to which he was so de-
voted, and Miss Yonge, the popular writer, gave
all the profits of her book, "The Daisy Chain,"
to the same work.

Bishop Selwyn's son was next made Bishop
of New Zealand, and he began his labors in
1877. His missionary ship was the Southern
Cross. In 1892 he had to resign his position on
account of ill-health, and the boat was replaced
by a fine steamer.

Native teachers now carry on the missions
among the islands throughout the year. During
the winter months European ministers live with
them to instruct and assist them a little, and to
open as many new doors as possible to the en-
trance of the gospel. Parts of the Bible have been
translated into the various languages. Many of
the islanders have been taught to read, a large
number have become members of the church,

and many young men have been trained to teach, several of them having become ministers.

The work on the Banks Islands has been marked by success. Some of the islands have been Christianized, and they are now under the charge of native pastors. In 1881 Santa Cruz showed itself open and friendly to the missionaries, and it now sends pupils to Norfolk Island.

The gospel has a good footing, too, on the Swallow Islands, and this mission has stations on some of the New Hebrides also.

On the Solomon Islands the natives are of the Papuan race, and have been in a low, savage state. The people of the northern islands have been said to be fiercer and more cruel than any of the tribes of the Pacific.

The name is supposed to have come from the fact that these islands have been conjectured to be the ones to which Solomon sent for his gold, ivory, apes and peacocks. The inhabitants build neat huts, make elaborate canoes, and are skilful in wood-carving and decorative work of inlaid shells and mother-of-pearl. A state canoe that belonged to the chief of one tribe was gracefully formed. Its stern-post rose like a mast, and it was beautifully ornamented. The canoe itself was made of bent planks cemented together by a kind of gum. This tribe worshipped a sacred image, or idol, which was

little more than a thick post, with a rude face
having inlaid rings for the eyes, two rows of
teeth for the mouth, and something on the sides
to represent ears.   In one island there are numerous huts built among the top branches of
high trees, to which the people climb by a sort
of rope-ladder, and in which they take refuge
from their enemies, defending themselves by
pouring down a volley of stones upon their pur-
suers. They have spears from ten to fifteen feet
long, with a point of sharp bone, for ordinary
fighting, and they use bows and arrows besides.
But even in this dark spot, among these head-
hunters and man-eaters, mission stations and
schools are now established, and these are largely owing to the influence of one of the boys of
the group, who was educated at Norfolk Island.
There are about nine thousand Melanesian Christians altogether.

In New Zealand at the present time there
are nearly two thousand churches and chapels,
besides many other buildings and houses in
which services are held.   The meetings are
attended by about one-third of the population.

Mr. Charles Darwin, the scientist, paid a visit
to the island of New Zealand, and this is what
he said when he came away: " The lesson of the
missionary is an enchanter's wand. I took leave
of the missionaries with thankfulness for their

welcome and high respect for their upright and useful characters."

A while ago a Hindu and a New Zealander met on board a ship. Each saw that the other was a Christian, because each carried a Bible, but they could exchange no ideas because they could not speak each other's language. Suddenly one of them smiled and said, " Hallelujah!" and the other man smiled back at him and responded with "Amen!" and then they felt that they understood each other. The change in New Zealand has been called "the standing miracle of the age."

CHAPTER VIII.

THE FIJI ISLANDS: THE PEOPLE AND THE LOTU.

WHEN the people of the Friendly Islands had learned the glad story of the Bible, they could not rest content with knowing it for themselves, but felt that they must pass it on to others; and where could it be more needed than in the neighboring islands of Fiji?

There was never a worse place than Fiji, so far as the people were concerned, although the islands and their surroundings were among the most beautiful in the southern seas. There are more than two hundred of these islands, eighty of which are inhabited. The rest are so small that many of them cannot be seen except at low tide. Most of them are encircled by coral reefs, which mark off, by a long line of white foam, the purple waves outside from the blue waters of the harbor within, and shine like rainbows up out of the ocean. Down through the clear water may be seen corals and seaweed of almost every tint, and fishes of brilliant hues dart here and there through the gay picture of color, which is varied continually by the ebb and flow of the tide and the shifting of light and shadow from above.

The natives were not altogether savages in spite of their wickedness and cruelty, for they were very clever about some things. They built very good houses, and they had unusual skill in the making of native cloth and pottery, and were adepts at the work of carving and basket-weaving. They say that their ancestors learned the art of pottery from the mason bee, and the common cooking and water vessels do, indeed, bear a close resemblance to the nests of these little creatures. The Fijians have no potter's wheel, but the labor is all performed by hand. Their cloth and their pottery are both decorated, often in artistic and elaborate patterns which are designed by the women.

The dwellers in the Fiji Islands are dark, but not black. It has been said that their shade is more like purple than like any other color. The dress of the men used to be made of a long piece of cloth, from three to one hundred yards in length, composed of pieces of tree-bark glued together and stained and figured in gay devices or in plain brown and white. This cloth would be wound round the hips and tied about the upper part of the body, the ends being left to trail behind. The women wore fastened round

the waist a band of roots or of bark and grass
with a deep fringe hanging from it.   Both men
and women adorned themselves with shell am-
ulets and finger-rings and with ornamental bands
at their knees and ankles.   They delighted in
necklaces of dogs' and sharks' teeth, and in those
made of the bones of bats and snakes.   Nearly
every man wore on his breast a large pearl shell
and a boar's tusk or two.   On their foreheads
many persons wore tufts of scarlet feathers,
and in their ears were thrust rings ten inches
around, or straight pieces as thick as their fingers or their wrists.   Sometimes they would fling
garlands of flowers or of vines across their
shoulders, as though they had not already made
themselves striking enough by tattooing themselves in designs in blue, or by burning patterns down their backs or upon their sides and
arms, or by painting their faces in grotesque
figures and glaring colors.   Their hair they
dyed in almost every shade, red being the
favorite tint among the young women.   Then
these disguised locks they would arrange in the
most unnatural and startling style possible ; the
chief aim seemed to be for each to make himself or herself as hideous as might be.   Some
of these heads when dressed would be three
feet around.   Some looked as though they were
bristling with stiff paint-brushes set on end.

Some were shaved all over except for a patch of hair on each side or one in front, and some would be shaved on top, while the hair that was left would be brushed up into a tall fan behind. Sometimes there would be a black mop at the back and a white roll in front, and sometimes the whole head would look as though it were covered with a crinkled worsted cap.

Each chief had his own hair-dresser, who would spend hours each day arranging his master's hair.

The Fijians were all cannibals of the lowest type. The man who had eaten the greatest number of human beings was thought the most worthy of regard, and a stone was set up by every one for every victim that was devoured by him. One chief had a long honor-roll of three hundred of these stones to mark his own cruelty. There were other customs, too, quite as bad as cannibalism. When a man died his widows were strangled and sent out of the world after him. Each wife of a chief always wore a strap around her neck, so that she might be ready to follow her husband at a moment's notice. Old and sick persons, and little children, too, were often killed in order that their friends might not be burdened with their support.

"Why should we let girls live?" asked one

chief. " What are they good for ?   They cannot swing a club or throw a spear !"

When the women were allowed to remain in the world they were simply slaves, and nobody cared much for them.   Neither had the men much consideration for the lives and property of one another. They were always at war, and there was no harm in stealing, they thought, so long as they were not caught in the act. To have the theft found out was indeed a disgrace, and the man who was so stupid as to let his misdeed be discovered was looked upon with contempt. The natives had a sort of belief in a great Power who had other gods under him and who made known his will to the priests ; and they had an idea that the spirits of their ancestors lived in the animals about them. They believed that every person had two spirits : one that left the body at death, and one that was seen in mirrors or was reflected in water. There was a temple in every village, but it served many other purposes besides those that were religious. There was no regular worship, and little heed was paid to the temple unless the chief wished to make some special request of the gods, when he would repair the building and bring an offering of food, and sometimes, when he was unusually anxious for the granting of some favor, even a number of whales' teeth. Whales' teeth were the most valued of all possessions in Fiji. One tooth would buy a whole man.

And this was Fiji, where those men who had earned their right to the name of their islands were about to go to work. They had not many missionaries themselves, those Friendly Islanders, but they decided in the large-hearted Christian way that they might spare two for their brothers in Fiji. They chose two of their very best, William Cross and David Cargill, who had come to them from the Wesleyan Church in Great Britain; and in the year 1834 the two men set sail for the abode of those of whom they had heard so much evil and so little good. During the voyage they spent most of their time in studying the new language that soon they would have to speak, but they could not do much with it in the four days that were taken in crossing the sea. They landed at Lakemba; but they had no introduction to the people of Fiji except that contained in a letter written to the chief by King George of Tonga, and that did not seem a very strong weapon just then with which to approach the crowd of painted savages, dancing and yelling on the beach, armed with clubs ten or fifteen feet long and battle-axes of hard wood. Still, the strangers made their way to the shore and forced themselves into the presence of the king, who read the letter and condescended to say that the missionaries might stay if they wished. He even promised to build houses for them.

That point was gained then, and the two men gratefully accepted the king's permission to live among his subjects, and went to work to see what could be done with the barbarians. They were interested in these new-comers, that was certain, and were curious about their homes and their ways, so unlike their own. They were willing to listen, too, to the words of the missionaries, and after a while a church was built, and the natives came to the services. But troubles there were, aud hindrances, and all manner of discouragement, of course. Was there ever a mission without its share of these? and wicked Fiji could not be reformed in a day. The crops of the teachers were destroyed, their goods were stolen, and they themselves were often in danger of losing their lives. Sometimes there were terrible cannibal-feasts close beside them, and they would have to shut themselves within their own homes, and pray, pray all night long, with sad hearts and distracted minds.

Frequently, also, they suffered from lack of food and clothing, and sometimes had to barter some of the few things that they had that were not mere necessities of life for just enough to eat to keep themselves alive.

POINT VENUS AND MATAVAI BAY, TAHITI.

But help was coming to these brave men.
Down in England were two young fellows,
named John Hunt and James Calvert, who were
going out as missionaries, and who thought that
this dreary, dingy little corner of the world
would be a good place to work in. So to Fiji
they came, in the year 1838. Even with this
addition to their force the missionaries had to
spread themselves over as much ground as possible. John Hunt was placed first at Rewa and
afterwards at Buwa, a small island on the eastern side of Great Fiji. James Calvert and his
faithful wife were settled at Lakemba.

The first thing that Mr. Calvert had to do
was to bury the heads, hands and feet of eighty
persons who had just been slaughtered for a cannibal feast. This was a heart-sickening opening
to his task, but he did not falter or fall back on
that account. He lighted his little candle in the
black night of heathenism and after a while it
made its glimmer seen. The latest comers had
brought a printing-press with them across the
sea, and the books and translations of parts of the
Bible that had been prepared by Mr. Cross and
Mr. Cargill were printed at once. Mr. Calvert
could not visit all the islands in his circuit, but
the people used to come from all around to Lakemba to buy goods, and they always stopped at
the mission-house for a call. Here they were al-

ways gladly welcomed, and they never failed to carry away something to think about and talk over.

So the light began to steal out from Lakemba to other islands, and the people began to ask for more beams from that candle set aflame by the Sun of Righteousness. Teachers were sent to them, and it really seemed, in many places, as though the poor natives had only been waiting for a little guidance in order to turn their faces towards the Light of the World. The " Lotu," they called the new religion, and many of them grasped it eagerly. Whole villages gave up their idols and humbly and patiently set out on the Christian path, that would shine for them more and more until the perfect day should dawn upon them.

On the island of Ono the people had been going through severe trials, coming from war and sickness, and they had been praying to their gods for aid. But no answers had been given them, and they were almost in despair, when one of their number heard in some way that the natives of the Friendly Islands said that there was but one God, whom everybody ought to serve, and that, moreover, one day in seven was especially set apart for his worship. The inhabitants of Ono at once made up their minds to go to this God for help, and to follow his wishes by keep-

ing one day sacred to him.   For several months
they clung steadfastly to this purpose, and then
their prayers found a response.   A canoe filled
with men from a Christian island was driven out
of its course by a storm—one of God's good
storms, that have done so much for the South
Sea folk—and this canoe brought them people
who could tell them that which they had been
longing to know.   When news of their need was
carried to Lakemba a teacher was sent to them,
and when he reached Ono he was greeted by
twenty persons who had given up idolatry and
were ready to take Christianity into their hearts.

A chapel was built, many converts were baptized, and of all the work in Fiji that done at
Ono has been the most gratifying.

CHAPTER IX.

THE FIJI ISLANDS. CANNIBALS CHANGED TO CHRISTIANS.

MR. CALVERT made one or two visits to Ono and was always encouraged by the good work that was going on in that island. At one time there was special interest among the people and whole days and nights were spent in praying and singing. One of the native converts said: "I am thankful to have lived until the Lord's work began. I feel it in my heart. I hold Jesus; I am happy. My heart is full of love to God."

But there was one place upon which the missionaries had fixed their gaze and on which their eyes were now resting with especial anxiety and desire. That place was Mbau, where lived the king Tanoa, who had great influence over the whole of Fiji. He was one of the most bloodthirsty rulers among all the Pacific Islands, but his son, Thokambau, in whose hands the government now really lay, was even worse than his father. He had been brought up to find his pleasure not in healthful sports, like ball or tennis, nor in the improving study of books and nature, nor in harmless occupations like stamp-collecting or bug-hunting. His amusement came from fighting and from killing people, in torturing his captives and watching their agonies, and his education was for the sake of making him familiar with all sorts of wicked heathen customs. His royal name was "Vuni Valu," which means "Root of War," and a very good name it was for the fierce prince.

"I hate your Christianity," he said to the missionaries. "Do you think that you can keep us from our wars and from eating men? *Never!*"

But the missionaries were praying for these bitter enemies of theirs with all their hearts, and they knew that there was Some One who was with them who was stronger than all those who were with Thokambau, even though as yet not one of the teachers had been allowed to settle at Mbau. Still they had some things to cheer them in their work: the king of Lakemba became a Christian, and another chief was converted who built a beautiful chapel at Lakemba.

In 1845 good John Hunt died, after ten years of toil among the Fijians. He was so weak in his last moments that he was forbidden to speak, but he could not keep quiet. "Oh, let me pray once more for Fiji," he begged. "O God, bless Fiji! Save Fiji! Thou knowest my soul has loved Fiji!"

The natives who had been under his care stood by in great distress at seeing their friend slipping away from them. One old war-chief prayed piteously, with the tears running down his cheek : " O Lord ! we know that we are very evil, but spare Thy servant. Take me, take ten of us, but spare Thy servant to preach Christ to the people."

It was time, however, for John Hunt to go to his reward, but his prayers for Fiji were not forgotten above.

Soon after Mr. Hunt's death Mr. Calvert moved over to Viwa, and soon the harvest began to be gathered in. During the eight following years great progress was made with the people. In 1853 a missionary named Waterhouse was really admitted to Mbau, and even those hard-hearted men, Tanoa and Thokambau, could not close their ears so tightly that some whisper of the wondrous message could not force its way in and refuse to be thrust out again. Still Thokambau would do nothing more than promise that he would pay some attention to the words of the teachers when he should have subdued all his enemies.

One day, when the missionaries were away from home, word was brought to their wives that some strangers had come to Fiji on a visit, and that fourteen women were to be sacrificed as

an offering in their honor, according to the Fiji
notions of hospitality. Two of these brave missionary women, Mrs. Calvert and Mrs. Lyth, resolved to stop this dreadful deed, if possible.
Each took a whale's tooth in her hand, which is
the usual present in Fiji when one has a favor to
ask of a king, and hurried away by canoe to the
island of Mbau, about two miles away. Women
are forbidden to enter the king's house, but
there was no time to pause to think about laws
then. Into the king's presence they rushed, held
out their gift, and made known their request.
The king was quite overcome by their daring,
but was so struck by their courage that he said
that they might have the lives of the women
who had not yet been killed, and five of the victims were saved.

When Tanoa died the missionaries tried to
persuade his son to leave out the ceremony of
strangling his wives, "for grass for lining his
grave," as the expression goes in Fiji. Mr.
Calvert even went so far as to offer to have one
of his fingers cut off, to follow the Fiji fashion
in mourning, if the custom were omitted, but
Thokambau insisted on carrying out the old
practice.

But even this "king of the cannibal islands"
was conquered at last. He had many misfortunes, one after another. He was defeated in

battle, his life was threatened by his foes, and he became sick and discouraged and humble. He declared that he would give up his idols and become a Christian. In 1854 he called a large mass-meeting at Mbau. The drums that were formerly used to announce a cannibal feast were now beaten to summon the people to church. Three hundred persons heard and accepted the invitation, and looked on in awe and wonder as the "Root of War" came in, accompanied by his wives, children, and relations, and knelt in worship before the Christian's God.

After this time he came regularly to the meetings, kept Sunday faithfully, and began to learn his letters. He was taught by his own little boy, who was only six years old ; but it was hard work to start on the task of forming acquaintance with the alphabet at the age of fifty, and poor old Thokambau often fell asleep during the lesson. In 1857 he did indeed become truly converted, and he was baptized under the name of Ebenezer. He must have been in earnest in his new life, for he stood up before all the people, whom he had made treat him almost as though he were a god, and owned all his old wickedness.

" I have been a bad man," he said. " The missionaries came and invited me to embrace Christianity, but I said to them, 'I will continue to fight.' God has singularly preserved my life. I desire to acknowledge him as the only and true God."

In 1874 Thokambau ceded the Fijian Islands to England, and in 1886 he died, a gentle, faithful, intelligent Christian. His club and the bowl that used to hold the native drink of which he had been fond he presented to Queen Victoria, and they may still be seen in the British Museum.

After eighteen years of labor Mr. Waterhouse also died. His last words were, " Missionaries! Missionaries! Missionaries!" During the period of his stay in Fiji the whole of the Bible was translated and many copies of the New Testament were circulated.

At last Mr. Calvert went back to England, leaving other missionaries in his place. In 1885 he paid a visit to his old field, and found it an entirely different place from what it was when he had first seen it. One hundred thousand people, out of a population of one hundred and twenty-five thousand, were Christian converts. There were two hundred chapels, over two thousand missionary preachers and teachers, and twenty-six thousand church-members. In all the eighty inhabited islands there was not a person who was called a heathen. James Calvert died in 1892.

On the island of Mbau there was once a large stone in front of the chief temple. Against this stone the bodies of victims were dashed, as an offering to the gods, before they were given over for the cannibal feasts. It has now been taken from its old position and placed as a baptismal font in the Mbau church, and for nearly forty years it has had upon it no new stain of human blood.

There are now about one thousand Wesleyan churches in Fiji. Eighty-three per cent. of the population is made up of church-members, and there are over one thousand preachers and over two thousand teachers. Every morning and evening may be heard the sound of hymns floating on the air and the low murmur of voices engaged in prayer.

It is easy to see that the people in Fiji are sincere in their Christian aims and desires by the hearty way in which they throw themselves into the task of giving the gospel to others. As we shall learn by and by, they have been quick to respond to the call from New Guinea. They have sent teachers to New Britain, and the light has begun to creep over to New Ireland too. A Wesleyan missionary, the Rev. George Brown, began a mission in New Britain in 1875. Many native teachers went with him, and though several were killed, others took their places, and their wives would not be left behind. One brave woman, who was urged not to risk her life in so savage a place, replied simply, " The outrigger must go with the canoe; I go with my husband."

Forty-one churches were built in New Britain, and six thousand persons go regularly to the services. There are nine hundred church-members, over one thousand Sunday-school scholars, and forty-five native preachers. In 1892 the people gave $150 to missions.

In Fiji $5,000 is the yearly offering for missionary work. One of the native collections was made up of the following articles, showing that each person gave as he was able: Seventy-six mats, twenty-four baskets, three bows with arrows, seven pieces of sandal wood, sixteen fans, sixty-two fine clubs, one pillow, thirty-one spears, eleven hand-clubs, four women's dresses, three pieces of native cloth, five water vessels, four combs, and one pig.

One is now as safe in Fiji as in any part of the world. There are no British troops there. The only protection needed is given by a handful of native police.

A sea-captain was once driven ashore on one of these islands and was much alarmed, as he expected to be devoured by cannibals without much warning. But to his surprise he was welcomed by men in civilized dress, who took him into their houses and treated him with all kindness and respect. When it was time to go to bed his host told him it was the hour for evening worship, and asked him to lead in prayer, but the captain had to confess that he did not know much about praying; so, to his shame, he had to kneel down and let the poor Fijian speak for him to his Father in heaven. He was so much impressed with the circumstances of this visit that he sought the Christian way for himself and became in time a missionary, and tried to teach others what had been taught him by a man who was once a cannibal.

There was another man who went to the Fiji Islands—an English earl and an infidel. He smiled in a superior manner when he met the natives.

"You are a great chief," he said to one of them, "and it is really a pity that you have been so foolish as to listen to the missionaries. Nobody believes any longer in that old book called the Bible, or in that story of Jesus Christ. They have all learned better. I am sorry for you, that you have been so foolish as to take it in."

The chief's eyes flashed as he replied, "Do you see that great stone over there? On that stone we smashed the heads of our victims to death. Do you see that native oven over yonder? In that oven we roasted the human bodies for our great feasts. Now if it had n't been for the good missionaries, and that old Book, and the love of Jesus Christ, which has changed us from savages into God's children, you would never leave this spot. You have to thank God for the Gospel; for without it here we should have killed you, and roasted you in yonder oven, and feasted upon your body in no time."

So we may say, with one of these changed Fijians, "Ask no more, What can the Lotu do? after what our eyes have seen this day. The Lotu is of God, and whatever we now see is the work of God."

There are a good many Hindoos now in the Fiji Islands, and missionary work has to be done among these people. It is interesting to know that a Hindoo convert from India, named John Williams, has gone to Fiji to labor among his countrymen.

CHAPTER X.

THE NEW HEBRIDES: LITTLE JOHNNIE GEDDIE.

THE New Hebrides Islands belong to the Melanesian group and number about forty islands, of which thirty are inhabited. They extend three hundred miles from southeast to northwest. The population is about one hundred thousand.

The natives are mostly Papuans, with dark skin and curly hair. They were once all cannibals, and they had no regard for human life, and of women they thought nothing at all. "It was only a girl, you know," said one man, carelessly, after he had confessed to having buried his own child alive. Still they must have wives, as they were convenient in many ways, but they bought them as they bought any other article for the household, paying for them with pigs, the number of pigs varying on the different islands in proportion as women were scarce or numerous. The people believed in a life after the death of the body, but were in continual fear of evil spirits and witches. They had many gods: gods of the sea, gods of the bush, and gods of everything. They believed, too, in men who, as they thought, had power over disease, over the wind, over the thunder, and over other forces of nature.

The first missionary who tried to reach these people was that untiring John Williams, who was murdered at that cruel little island of Erromanga.

On hearing of his death twenty-five men at once offered themselves as missionaries, and the Christians in England made up their minds that the New Hebrides must be won for Christ. The missionaries at Samoa managed to station teachers at Erromanga, and at some other islands, but they could not stay long, strong and steadfast as they were. Some of them died, and the rest gave up the work in despair. In 1841 Mr. Murray left some teachers at Aneityum, and in 1842 Mr. Turner and Mr. Nisbet went to Tanna; but Tanna was not yet ready for the gospel, and the missionaries were driven away. In 1845 another attempt was made, and some teachers were placed there, and later four natives from the islands were taken to the Missionary Institute at Samoa, given three years' training, and then sent home to do what they could among their countrymen. Then good Bishop Selwyn would call occasionally in his mission boat.

The natives of the island of Aneityum are somewhat different from the other inhabitants

of Eastern Polynesia.   They are small, dark, and
slender, and lack the spirit and energy of many
of the South Sea Islanders.   The climate of the
island is like June all the year round.   Bananas,
cocoanuts and yams grow there in abundance,
and there is no lack of bread-fruit, sandal-wood,
sugar-cane and arrowroot.   There are no wild
beasts, and no poisonous snakes, and nothing
was savage or unlovely except the people.   But
the people!   They seemed to some persons to
be too little like men, and too much like animals, for anything to be done for them.   But
God had a man ready for even a place like
this.   Not a strong, athletic man, like Bishop
Selwyn or John Coleridge Patteson, but a fine
man for all that—a man with a big heart, full
of the love of God and his fellow-man, and one
who, giving all diligence, added to his faith
virtue, and patience, and many other traits of
which Peter has written.

   " Little Johnnie Geddie " he was called when
he was a boy at home in Nova Scotia, and used
to pore over the stories of the heroes of the
South Seas until he was filled with their spirit,
and was glowing with a great desire to do as
they had done.   He would be a missionary, too,
he told his mother, and steadily did he hold to
his purpose.   Through striving and self-denial
he managed to get an education, and then he

had to win his way into the work on which he
had set his heart.

With his old horse, whose name was Sam-
son, he started on a tour round the country and
talked missions wherever he went. People listened to him because they could not help listening. The young man was so earnest, and so
determined, and so burning with his subject,
that the churches were all stirred too, and
they agreed to raise enough money for his support in his chosen field.

Then he gave himself up to studying medicine and to learning other useful things. He
found out how to build a house, and a boat, and
then felt as though he might venture out to his
work.

At last he set forth, on a small brig, on a
long journey, of nineteen thousand miles, round
Cape Horn to the Sandwich Islands. At this
place he stayed several weeks, and then was off
to the Samoan group. At Samoa he lingered
for two months, during which time he learned
the Samoan language, and then the John Williams took him with another missionary, whose
name was Powell, over to the New Hebrides.

They decided to begin work at Ancityum,
but they were not as warmly welcomed as they
might have been. "You must n't hurt the
white men," said the chief, Nohoat, to his fol-

lowers, " but you may steal from them as much as you like, and by and by they will be tired and go away."

But Mr. Geddie had no mind to fall in with this arrangment. He built a house and then set at work at the language. He could not make the natives talk at first, but by offering each one a biscuit for each word that he said he succeeded in coaxing away from them some knowledge of their speech. This was certainly an easy way of earning one's living, but perhaps the plan sometimes cost Mr. Geddie his own meal. When he had gained enough of the language to make himself understood he started out to explore his island, and on this tour he preached at every point where he stopped—sometimes under the trees, sometimes by the sea-shore—and when he went home he sent teachers to go on with the work he had begun. Then he held regular services at his first station and the people came to the meetings, although they really thought they should be paid for doing so.

For a while everything seemed to be doing well, when a sudden change came over the natives. They stole from the missionaries more frequently than ever, and abused their belongings. One of the sacred men of the island, who had the remarkable title of " The man who rules the sea," said that the reason for this conduct was that Mr. Geddie was using his cocoanuts instead of saving them for the sacred feasts, and that the gods were displeased because he had taken coral for his house and so they had driven away the fish ; and besides he had built a fence in the way of the gods, so that they could not reach the sea, and as their wrath had fallen on the islanders and brought them disease and death the natives were revenging themselves upon the strangers.

John Geddie was too kind and sensible to laugh at the ignorant natives for their foolish notions. He tried to yield to their whims so far as possible, and by his gentleness and generosity he kept his influence over them and was all the time gaining a little more. But they were very suspicious and superstitious, and very fond of fighting, so that they were always falling into their old ways and having to be pulled out again.

When the island was visited by a hurricane Nohoat said that it was caused by one of their wonder-workers, called "The wind-maker," and he tried to kill him. This brought on a war and Mr. Geddie had to be peace-maker. He stepped bravely in between the two parties drawn up for battle and told them that it was Jehovah only who ruled the clouds, and that He would be displeased with them if they should fight about his actions. At last the natives agreed that they would hold a council over the matter, and the chiefs made up the quarrel by giving each other a spear and piece of cloth.

Next all the missionaries fell ill, and the natives declared that the gods were now indeed angry with them. Only a few persons would come to church, and those who were present at the meetings did not behave very well. Some of them would use the opportunity for a comfortable little nap, and some would smoke their pipes, and some would run away before the service was half over. Mr. Powell's health gave out altogether, and when the John Williams touched at the island he seized the chance to go back to Samoa.

For three years John Geddie was alone among the savages, except for his wife and three little children, but he kept bravely on with his work. He printed a book of twelve pages, and started both a boys' and a girls' school. The natives began to come to church again after a while, and as time passed on four prominent men gave up their idols and became Christians. Then the people all took the missionary into favor and wished to make him a chief. More natives turned away from heathenism, and the converts went out and preached to their neighbors in other parts of the island.

Nothing was stolen now ; no clubs nor spears came to church, but the people were there without them. Attentive and reverent they were too ; and indeed they were so anxious now to be like their friend Mr. Geddie that they felt that they must be dressed like him. But on the whole island there was not enough of the kind of clothing that he wore to supply everybody, so the natives hit upon a plan to make it go round. One article would be passed from one member of a family to another, so that each one might have a turn at wearing it one Sunday at least. Sometimes this precious bit of raiment would be only a scrap of an old sail, but it was eagerly put on, as being as near to a white man's garment as anything that they could find.

The heathen party at last became alarmed, and resolved to bring to an end all this interest in the new religion. Nohoat, the chief, promised Mr. Geddie that he should not be hurt ; they only wished to sweep away all the native Christians. But if Mr. Geddie's converts were touched he was touched too, and in a very tender spot.

"If you make war on my Christians," said he, "we will all go away to another island."

Now that was not to the liking of the old chief. He felt that it was a great distinction to have a missionary all to himself, on his own island; and, besides, what should he do for medicine and the other useful things that went with the missionaries?

He would wait a while before stirring up strife, after all, he thought; but in little underhand ways the converts were persecuted all the time by their heathen neighbors, and Mr. Geddie's life was often threatened. In the midst of everything he fell ill; but his loving disciples were so faithful and brave and steadfast that he was comforted and helped in his trials, and at last the clouds blew over. A sickness from which the Christians were free broke out among the heathen, and some of them began to think that perhaps they had been mistaken in supposing that the Christian religion brought them trouble, and they were glad enough to have that good Christian, John Geddie, at hand just then with his little stock of remedies.

Another of the medicine-men was converted, and as he at once began to teach others the number of Christians grew from day to day. Parts of the Bible were printed in the language of the island, and in spite of the enmity and evil influence of the sandal-wood traders then on Aneityum the gospel kept on spreading. One man stretched out his arms and then brought his hands together, saying, " The word of God is like this; it has gone round the island."

Even Nohoat showed that he was dropping some of his old ideas, by eating food forbidden to chiefs, and "Father Geddie," as he was called, was authority on almost every subject. Whenever there was a disagreement he had to settle it, and his advice had to be given in many matters. The sacred groves were cut down and the sacred stones were scattered.

Mr. Geddie was so busy that he wrote home and begged for a missionary to be sent out to help him, but no missionary came. Then his supplies gave out, and he would have had no bread at all if some shipwrecked sailors had not shared some mouldy bread with him. He was sick, too, but he had no time to devote to rest and nursing, for he had to bolster himself up in bed and prepare doses for others.

The John Williams had not been seen for two years and a half, but when the boat did appear at last how gladly was it greeted!

The Samoans who came with it could hardly believe their eyes when they saw what a change had passed over the island in four years. The language had been learned and reduced to writing, and thousands of books were in the hands of the people, hundreds of whom could read them. Hundreds of children were in school, half of the four thousand people on the island had been brought to Christ, and a little church had been formed which had fifteen members. This was the first church of the Papuan race.

Soon afterwards Bishop Selwyn and Coleridge Patteson arrived bringing with them a new missionary, the Rev. John Inglis. He was placed upon the other side of the island, where he did the same kind of work that John Geddie had done on this side.

After a while Simeona and Pita, the two teachers who had been the first missionaries at Aneityum, moved over to Tanna to see what could be done there, and two or three years afterwards the old chief Nohoat, who had become a Christian, went forth on the same errand.

The natives at Aneityum built a house for Mr. Geddie, and a large church which would hold one thousand people. Chapels and school-houses were scattered all over the island. A form of government was established, and a law was passed forbidding the women to be sold as slaves. More land was cultivated, and the people began to export arrowroot and other products.

After fifteen years of service Mr. Geddie went home for a short vacation, returning to Aneityum after a year's absence. But the climate and the work and the care had broken his constitution, and in 1872 he died, at the age of

fifty-eight. On a simple tablet in his church is
this inscription : " When he landed in 1848 there
were no Christians here, and when he left in
1872 there were no heathen."

Nobody could wish to leave a nobler record
than that shown in these words.

The Rev. Mr. Murray took up the work at
Aneityum. That was already firmly established,
but over in Erromanga the struggle to plant the
banner of the cross was still going on.

The Rev. George Gordon, from Prince Ed-
ward's Island, had begun work in 1857, and had
met the same sort of trials that had befallen
Geddie at Aneityum, though with a less happy
result.

In 1861 there was a hurricane on the island
and an epidemic of measles as well, both of
which misfortunes were, of course, laid at the
door of the foreigners, and the natives fell upon
Mr. Gordon and his wife and murdered them
both. Bishop Patteson, who stopped at the isl-
and soon afterwards, read the burial-service over
their bodies, not thinking, perhaps, that he
would soon fall in the same manner himself.

Three years later George Gordon's brother
James reached the spot where the dreadful deed
had been done, hoping to be able to go on with
the work that his brother had started. In 1867 he
was joined by James Mac Nair, from Scotland,

who died in 1870, leaving the first James alone again.

One day when he was sitting on the veranda of his own home, revising the translation of the seventh chapter of Acts, which tells of the death of Stephen, a native came creeping up with his tomahawk and laid another victim low. Like Stephen, he had died a martyr to the cause that he loved.

Now it did seem as though Erromanga were a hopeless field and all labor bestowed upon her were worse than wasted; but then out stepped another heroic soul, saying, "Here am I; send me!"

Hugh Robertson was his name, and he, too, was from Nova Scotia. He had once read a little book written by Mr. Gill, one of the Samoan missionaries, called "Gems from the Coral Isles," and these stories had taken so strong a hold of his fancy, and so touched his heart, that nothing seemed to him worth doing except going out as a missionary to people like those about whom he had read. Now James Gordon was about to sail from Halifax about the time that young Robertson was turning over this matter in his mind, so the latter resolved to go with him and see for himself what missionary work was like. He was taken to Aneityum, where he lived for four years and a half, keep-

ing his keen eyes open to judge fairly what
heathenism really was when one saw it close at
hand, with all the romance rubbed off.   But
what he found, though worse than he had
imagined, only made him more eager than ever
to engage in a conflict with evil; but it made
him feel, too, that he needed more preparation
for the fight.   He went home, took a course in
theology and a course in medicine, and then
was ready for the call to Erromanga — Erromanga that killed all the prophets that were
sent unto her and would not be helped by anybody.

But God had not given up Erromanga, so
why should his servant, Hugh Robertson?   It
was in 1872 that he set sail with his wife for the
New Hebrides.   Even the sailors on the ship
were afraid to stay near the land, so they hastily
placed their passengers upon the shore and hurried away as fast as they could.   It must have
been a strange, thrilling moment for the two
deserted beings when they saw the vessel dis-
appear in the distance, and knew that they
themselves were now beyond human knowledge
and human aid.   After a while some natives
appeared and stared at them in surprise.   They
could speak a little English, and after a few moments of parleying they consented to conduct
the strangers to the mission-house, which had

been surrounded by a stockade for the protection of the former inhabitants. There the savages left their guests for a time, but before long back they came, armed with clubs, looking fierce and angry and like anything but hospitable hosts. Mr. Robertson stepped out upon his veranda and told them quietly and pleasantly that he himself could do nothing against them, of course, but that Jehovah, his God, had him in charge, and if they should injure him they would have an account to settle with God. They listened to these words, looked at each other, and then slunk away. They were afraid of the One whom the Christians worshipped.

Still, when their wicked feelings rose again, they hurried back, fully resolved to rid themselves of these white people who had forced themselves upon them. Once more Mr. Robertson met them with the same calm words, and once more they gave up their purpose and went meekly home. Over and over did they go through this performance, but at last they seemed to tire of these visits, and were willing to have the missionaries among them. Mr. Robertson lived with them for a year, and then summoned the chiefs for a consultation.

"Now," said he, "I have been here for a good while. You have seen that I am your friend and that I have tried to help you. If you will treat me well, and stop trying to kill me, I will stay with you longer. If not, I will go away at once. You must decide for yourselves."

The chiefs withdrew, and talked the matter over. "Let us kill him at once," said one, "and be rid of him." "No," said another, "let him be here with us; he does no harm"; and so they reasoned, back and forth, until the friendly party carried the day, and word was sent to the missionaries that they were to be allowed to remain. After this favor on their part the natives seemed to lose many of their objections to the outsiders, and adopted them as their charge. They began to listen to their teaching, too, and love and devotion were not without their reward.

During the following year many persons were converted, and in eleven years the island was won. At the close of 1882 five hundred Erromangans went regularly to church, and one hundred and ninety of them were church-members. Then, as he had thirty-three native teachers to carry on the work at various stations throughout the island, Mr. Robertson felt that he might go home for a visit. As he was about to depart, an old chief lifted a little child in his arms and said, "When I was the age of this baby there was not a Christian on this island. When he is my age, there will not be one heathen."

Perhaps he had heard of Mr. Geddie's inscription at Aneityum, or perhaps the facts in this case were as plain as they were in the other, so that the same expression came naturally into mind.

In 1880 a church was dedicated at Dillon's Bay, not far from the spot where John Williams fell. It was called "The Martyrs' Memorial Church." Not long afterwards the natives paid for having one thousand copies of the "Acts of the Apostles" printed and gave generously to the fund for publishing the four Gospels, designed for circulation among the people. There are now about twenty-five hundred Christians on the island, in thirty-four villages. There are schools and teachers in every part, and church services are held every Wednesday and Sunday.

In the Memorial Church may be seen the following inscription:

Sacred to the memory of Christian missionaries who died on this island:

JOHN WILLIAMS,
JAMES HARRIS,

Killed at Dillon's Bay by the natives,
30th November, 1839.

GEORGE N. GORDON,
ELLEN C. GORDON,

Killed on the 20th of May, 1861.

JAMES MacNAIR,

Who died at Dillon's Bay, 16th July, 1870;
and
JAMES D. GORDON,

Killed at Portinia Bay, 7th March, 1872.

They hazarded their lives for the sake of the
Lord Jesus.

In 1889, the fiftieth anniversary of the death
of John Williams, a monument was erected at
Erromanga. The man who laid its corner-stone
was the son of his murderer, and another son of
this same savage was at the time preaching the
gospel in Australia.

CHAPTER XI.

THE NEW HEBRIDES: THE MAN WHO DUG THE WELL.

ABOUT ten years after John Geddie went to Aneityum, and shortly after George Gordon had made an attack on Erromanga, that man who has become so famous among missionary heroes, Dr. John G. Paton, fell into the same line of work at Tanna.

There is a volcano on Tanna which gives the island the name of the " Lighthouse of the South Pacific," but we know very well that Tanna was not a light in the way of morals or of manners. Dark, very dark, was it in Tanna in those respects, and every spark of the gospel glow had been dashed out just as soon as it had been kindled.

But John Paton was willing to give Tanna another trial.

He was another one who had made up his mind when he was a little boy that he would be a missionary so soon as he was old enough; and his home in Scotland, where he grew up under the care of one of the wisest and best fathers and one of the loveliest mothers that ever lived, must have been just the sort of place

TAHITIAN GIRLS, TAHITI.

from which to send out a good missionary. He must have drunk in high thoughts and aims with the mountain air and learned patience and steadfastness from the hills, while from his father and mother he gained much of his simple trust, his industry and thrift, his courage and his hardihood, as well as his bright, hopeful disposition and kind, warm heart. Yet from all the beauty of his native land, and from all the home ties and associations, he turned away to cast in his lot among the savages of Tanna.

He found the people cannibals, like all the natives of the New Hebrides. They lived in poor little huts, the men spending their time in fighting while the women did the work. They had many idols and worshipped almost everything, after the way of their neighbors.

They allowed Mr. Paton and his companions to stay with them because they thought that they would give them axes and fish-hooks, and making the most of this permission Mr. Paton tried to become acquainted with them, and to learn their language while he was working his way into their lives. One day he noticed that a man picked up some object that was new to him and said, inquiringly, " Nunski nari enu?" That must mean, " What is it?" thought Mr. Paton, quickly, and then he put his lesson into practice. He caught up some article and hold-

ing it out towards a savage he smiled and asked;
" Nunski nari enu?"   The native at once replied
with the name of the thing that Mr. Paton had
in his hand, and from that time " Nunski nari
enu?" brought the missionary a good deal of in-
formation.

Next he laid hold of the children and taught
them to sing. The music pleased the older people so much that they wished to learn how to
make it too, so Mr. Paton had a singing-class of
men and women. By means of the hymns he
was able to put into their minds ideas that would
have been difficult for them to grasp in any
other way. The first hymn that he gave them
spoke of God the Father, the second one of Jesus
Christ, and the third of the Holy Spirit; and
when they were curious about the meaning of
what they were singing he would explain to
them, as simply as he could, as much Bible
truth as they could understand.

But they were just as superstitious and as
suspicious as the people of Aneityum, and when
the rain came when it was not wished, or failed
to appear when they thought that it should, it
was all the fault of the missionary and his
friends. " Missi," they called him, in their child-
like fashion, and " Missi " was to them a wonderful being. When they laid plans to kill him he
seemed to know it, and to be prepared for them.

"How can you tell, Missi, what we mean to do to you?" they would ask, innocently.

"Oh, a little bird whispers it to me," he would answer, with a smile.

"What kind of a bird is it, Missi?" they would go on, still more puzzled than ever.

But Mr. Paton would only smile again, and leave them to guess that the bird was one of the children of whom he was so fond, and who loved him in return.

He did gain some influence over the older people too after a while. They were afraid of him, and were often so angry with him that they would gladly have murdered him, but he interested them, and they could not fail to respect him and to enjoy his kindness and his help in time of need. He often broke off a war when they were bent on fighting, and at one time ran into the midst of a party gathered together to talk over the coming battle, and called out: "My love to all you men of Tanna! Fear not. I am your friend. I have come to tell you about Jehovah God, and good conduct such as pleases him."

One of the men led him to a seat and the savages danced about him like madmen, flourishing their knives and clubs in a frightful manner; but when this performance was over they consented to hold a second council on the sub-

ject of the war, and finally agreed to give it up
for the time.   This peace lasted for four months,
and Mr. Paton felt that they had really made a
long stride in the progress of civilization when
they could lay by their weapons for a whole
third of a year.

But his trials were by no means over.   His
wife and his little child both died, and his own
life was more than once almost brought to an
end by an axe or a gun in savage hands.

Sometimes a friendly native would interfere,
sometimes Mr. Paton himself would talk to the
men and make them ashamed of their evil notions.   Sometimes they felt some power about
him that filled them with awe and held them in
check.   Perhaps they had a dim vision of the
One who walked with the three men in the fiery
furnace ; for Mr. Paton said of himself : "I had
my nearest and dearest glimpses of the face and
smile of my blessed Lord in those dread moments when musket, club or spear was levelled
at my life."   He felt that he must have a church,
and built one, largely by the labor of his own
hands.   The wood came from Aneityum, and
was paid for by fifty pairs of trousers, sent to
him for the purpose by his old mission-class in
Glasgow.

Only five men, three women and three children came to the first service after the church

was ready, but that made a beginning, and that afternoon Mr. Paton visited ten villages and preached in each one. A great deal of his time was spent in caring for the sick, and he was both doctor and nurse.

At last six stations were established along the coast and placed under the care of teachers from Aneityum. But as the consciences of the people awoke they became uneasy, and were sorry that these strangers had come to spoil all the good, old comfortable easy times. Then, sad to say, a trading-vessel came to the island and blew all the little flames of discontent into a great blaze.

"The only way to deal with these savages," said the savages of the trading-ship, "is to sweep them off the face of the earth. We will manage them for you," and then they put on shore several men who had the measles, and left them to scatter the disease. It spread like fire over the island and the natives fell rapidly before it. Thirteen persons from the mission party also died.

The people were roused to fury. They did not stop to think that the missionaries had suffered as well as themselves. They were full of hatred for all white men, and they would destroy any upon whom they could lay hands. To add to the commotion a hurricane tore over the island, and now the natives knew that the gods were surely angry, and would have the visitors at Tanna removed without delay.

One chief, whose name was Nowar, stood by Mr. Paton, but everybody else had turned against him. Everything was forgotten except that he belonged to the wicked race of white men, and time after time was he attacked. Every night bands of men prowled round the house, and Mr. Paton and his fellow-worker had to sleep with their clothes on, in readiness for a sudden flight.

They stuck to their post so long as there was a shadow of hope of doing any good there, but at last they were forced to believe that the work must be given up at Tanna for the present. One night, with nothing but their Bibles, their Tannese translations and a pair of blankets they slipped away, and after many adventures and hairbreadth escapes they reached the village of Nowar, on another part of the island.

Here they found the people in a state of terrible excitement. Crowds of armed men were seen bearing down upon them from every direction. They begged Mr. Paton to begin to pray for them as hard as he could, for they felt that they were lost. In his usual unruffled manner the good missionary turned, like a little child, to his Father, and asked for help. The savages were still pressing forward. On they came, until they were about three hundred yards away, when suddenly, and with no apparent reason, they wheeled round and walked off to their own village.

Two days Mr. Paton stayed with Nowar, but then even Nowar was afraid to have him longer in the house, so the next night the hunted man had to go out and climb into the arms of a tall chestnut-tree and there he spent the long hours until morning. All the time he could hear below him the cries of the savages and the popping of their muskets.

The following day Mr. Paton had another exciting journey, going this time to Mr. Matheson's station on the opposite side of the island. Here he waited ten days, hoping that a vessel might come and take him away One night he awoke to find the church on fire, and he saw, too, that the fence that connected it with the house was also in a blaze. He ran out and cut down one end of the fence, but then the natives were upon him. "Kill him! kill him!" they shrieked.

But just then there was a rumbling sound from the south. A hurricane was coming! The savages took fright at once.

"It is Jehovah's rain," they cried, and fled like dry leaves before the wind.

The next morning a ship from Aneityum touched at the island, and bore all the mission-aries away.

Mr. Paton went to Australia and to England and Scotland, and told about the work that must be done in the New Hebrides, ungrateful and unpromising though the people were. He suc-ceeded in raising money enough to buy a mis-sion-boat, most of it coming from children in Sunday-schools. The children's boat it was, that "white-winged angel," as Mr. Paton called the beautiful little vessel that had been named the Dayspring, and when it began to cruise among the islands the natives were filled with surprise. "Why, how is this?" they cried. "We have killed some of the missionaries and driven the others away. If we had been treated so nothing could bring any of us back. And is it to trade or get money, like other white men? No, but it is to tell us of their Jehovah God, and of his Son, Jesus. If their God makes them do all that we may well worship him too."

Mr. Paton and his new wife settled at Aniwa, a small island about nine miles long and three and a half miles wide. The language was not the same as that of Tanna, so he had to go to studying again. His experiences were much the same at first as those that had been met on the other island. The natives blamed the missiona-

ries for all their misfortunes, and thought that
the gods would like to have them put out of the
way. He visited many of the villages, and at
the risk of his life he told the people the story of
God's love. Sometimes he could protect himself
only by running straight into the arms of some
cannibal, and by clinging tightly around him
keep him from lifting his hand to strike with his
club or to fire with his gun. Sometimes he
would knock up the barrel of the musket pointed
at him, and send the bullet in another direction.

An old chief, Namakei, was converted, and
he was a great help to the missionaries. He
brought his daughter to be taught, and that was
the beginning of a school that trained many
young persons for service among their fellow-
men. The older people were much hurt because
they received no rewards for going to church,
and because the missionaries would not buy
their idols from them, so they tried to revenge
themselves in various ways. One night the old
chief, Namakei, came running into the missionaries' house, crying, " Rise, Missi, and help! The
heathen are trying to burn your house. All
night we have tried to keep them off, but they
are many, and we are few. Rise quickly, and
set a lamp in every window. Let us pray to Jehovah, and talk loud, as if we were many. God
will make us strong."

The woods were full of savages with lighted torches, but near the house the teachers and some friendly natives were keeping watch with buckets of water, ready to put out the fire should one be started. No harm was done, however, and when the day dawned the enemy slunk away.

There is little rain on the island of Aniwa, and all that falls soon sinks into the soil. There was one place called the "public water-hole," which was on the ground of some of the "sacred men," and which was filled by the rain. But these men pretended that they had the management of the weather, and would promise to bring a supply of water only when they were bribed with presents. So, of course, there was much suffering among the people for lack of good water.

Mr. Paton said that he meant to have a well of his own, from which anybody might help himself, but the people laughed at his idea. How could he bring rain up out of the ground? Rain came from above, they said.   But Mr. Paton went to work to dig. He coaxed the natives to help him by paying them with fish-hooks, but they became frightened, when one side of the hole caved in, and no more of that kind of work would they do. The gods were angry with them, they thought; but Mr. Paton toiled on alone.

They begged him to give up the job. "If you do reach water," said they, "you will fall through into the sea, and the sharks will eat you. We wonder what will be the end of this mad work!"

Still he dug away. The coral and earth were becoming damp. His hopes rose as his hole grew deeper. "I think God will give us water to-morrow," he said, one night.

Early the next morning he went down into his well and sank a small hole in the bottom. The water rushed in and overflowed it in a moment. He was so happy that he could hardly steady his hand while he tasted it from a cup that he had taken with him, but he eagerly sipped the water himself, and then, filling a jug that he had brought down empty, he carried it to the top of the well and showed it to the natives.

They fell back in wonder. Yes. It certainly was rain, though at first they dared not touch it. At last the old chief ventured to shake it, to see if it would spill, and laid his finger upon it, to learn if it felt like real water. Then he took some into his mouth and rolled it round there, finally letting it slip down his throat, and then shouting, "Rain! rain! Yes, it is rain!"

Then all the men had to peer down the well, and they were all "weak with wonder," as they said, at this marvellous event. They were ready

then to help to bring blocks of coral with which
to build a wall from top to bottom of this well
that had brought them rain from under the
ground.

The next Sunday Namakei preached a sermon in which he told the people that the "in-
visible Jehovah God" was the only God, and
they must throw away their idols and worship
him.   He had not only sent them rain from the
earth, but had given his Son from heaven to die
for them.   That same day many idols were
brought to Mr. Paton, and in the course of a few
weeks many more were piled at his door, and
they were then burned.   Then the people began
to wear the clothing of white men and women,
to go to church regularly, and to keep Sunday.
Mr. Paton had a book printed for them and they
were amazed to think that he could "make a
book speak."   They were still more overcome
when he began to teach them how to make it
speak to them also.

Next, they united in building a little church.
It was a queer little church, made of coral and
sugar-cane, with mats on the floors for seats ; but
it was just as good for their purposes.   They
were used to sitting on the ground.

Old Namakei devoted himself to the work of
helping the missionaries, and when he heard
how the gospel tidings were spreading he would

say, "Missi, I am lifting up my head like a tree;
I am growing tall with joy." When he died his
daughter said that he had been among all the
people and had charged them to be true to the
missionaries and to the cause of Christ, and that
they had promised to try to obey his words.

After three years of labor the first commu-
nion service was held in the little church. It
was a happy moment for the brave, loving heart
that had worked and waited so long; when the
dark hands were stretched out for the bread and
wine of the Lord's supper it was well-nigh broken
with bliss.

Then schools were established in various
parts of the island. These schools had to be
opened at daybreak, so that the men and women
might study their lessons before going out to
their day's work. Teachers were trained, and
the people were taught to do many useful things.
The Bible was translated and copies were given
out. Now there are thirty-five hundred Christians on Aniwa and two hundred native teachers.
Missionaries are no longer needed there.

Mr. Paton has said that it has been estimated
that one soul has been saved for every five dol-
lars spent in the work of the New Hebrides, and
Mrs. Paton says that it is worth laboring a life-
time to witness the change that comes over any
one of these people, even in the expression of the

face, when transformed from a savage into a Christian.

Tanna, too, is reaching out her hands towards the light. The natives who had been converted there were joined afterwards by other teachers, and through their efforts about fourteen hundred Christians have been gained even in Tanna. The best of it is that every convert is a missionary, so the work will go on.

On a small deserted island near Tanna Mr. Paton found on a recent visit that the people were trying to keep Sunday, though no missionary had been near them. Two old men kept track of the days, and on the first day of each week they would lay aside their ordinary occupations and each one would put on a calico shirt that he had, and then, calling the people round them, they would tell them as much as they knew of the gospel story. Upon inquiry Dr. Paton discovered that, thirty-three years before, he had stopped at this island for a week or so, and at that time had taught some of the people a little of the Bible and given out two calico shirts. Through all these long years these two men had cherished these bits of knowledge and carefully kept the shirts, wearing them only once in seven days in order to be able to make some difference between Sunday and the rest of the week. They further observed the day by doing the only other thing that seemed to them to belong to the occasion—sharing with others their own scanty portion of truth.

On Tonga, the Rev. Oscar Michelson toiled alone for twelve years At first he had many perilous adventures, and often had to run away and hide somewhere in order to save his life, but he kept at work, and the people liked him better after a while.   His home they called the " Sunday House," and they began to gather there to hear the music, and learned to sing some Christian hymns.   Then the work grew, and all over the island the good news was told.   Now there are thirty Christian teachers settled in various parts of the island, and Mr. Michelson's field includes three islands besides his own.   At one meeting lately three hundred persons rose for prayer.   The people of Tonga are now so honest that if one of them should find a coin on the road he would stick it up in some conspicuous place and there it would stay until the rightful owner should come along.

Fortuna was converted through the work of teachers from Aneityum. Some of the medicine men here when they became Christians brought their sacred stones, which they value above their lives, and burned them in the public square. Last year nine casks of arrowroot were sent to Edinburgh by the people of Aneityum, and three casks by the Christians in Fortuna. The latter contribution was to pay the expenses of building the first church in Fortuna. These people were so hungry for Bibles that they were willing to buy them at the rate of $2 a leaf.

Efaté, Malo and Nguna all have missionaries now, and a new mission has been started on the largest island, Espirito Santo. The second Dayspring has been sold and a small steamer has been provided in its place. About twenty islands are now occupied, and there are about fourteen thousand converts altogether. Portions of the Bible have been translated into fifteen distinct languages. There are about forty thousand cannibals in the New Hebrides that are still unreached, and for these Dr. Paton asks the prayers and the aid of Christians all over the world. He is anxious, too, to gain the sympathy and the help of the Christian nations in putting down the slave-trade in these islands, and in forbidding the bringing in by traders of rum, opium and fire-arms. These things are doing untold harm among the natives.

Dr. Paton has been able to devote the sum of $25,000 to his work from the proceeds of the book in which he has told the story of his life, and he has lived to have the pleasure of seeing one of his sons go back as a missionary to the New Hebrides, and another one is making ready to go.

CHAPTER XII.

THE SANDWICH ISLANDS: A COUNTRY OPENED BY A BOY.

The Sandwich Islands and Micronesia cannot be said to belong to the islands of the South Seas, as they lie north of the Equator, but they do make part of what is known as Polynesia, so their story is properly included with the other groups of that division.

The Sandwich Islands were named in 1778, by Capt. Cook, in honor of the Earl of Sandwich. There are ten of these islands, of which Hawaii is generally said to be the largest. It is, at least, the one of which we generally hear the most, and it now gives its name to the whole group.

About seventy years ago the inhabitants of these islands were savages and idolaters, and were wild, rough, and ignorant. All that they knew about civilization was what they had learned from the sailors on the ships that came occasionally to these shores. Their homes were grass huts, in which the natives and the animals lived together, and where the pig was an important member of the family.

Their religion was a mass of superstition.

Their idols were among the most hideous ever formed, and they had so many queer notions about everything that they could have found little comfort or pleasure in living. They believed that certain places or objects were sacred, or " tabu," as they said ; and if anybody should break any of the rules of " tabu " he was at once put to death. Some kinds of fish might be eaten by men, but were thought to be too good for women. A man was not allowed to eat with his wife, or a mother with her son; and the poor natives had an idea that the gods were so particular about such matters that if any offense were not speedily punished they would take the case into their own hands, and send to the whole group of islands some great calamity.

On the island of Hawaii is Kilauea, the largest volcano on earth. The crater is nine miles round, and one thousand feet deep. It is on the flank of the mountain of Mauna Loa, at an elevation of four thousand feet. In this volcano, the people of the island believed, lived Pele, the goddess of fire. The old stories said that she had made her home on one island after another, from each of which she had been driven by the water-god, Kamapuaa, who had the body of a man and the head of a pig. At last she had taken refuge in the volcano of Kilauea, and whenever she was angry she would turn into a flow of lava and rush down upon the people, or throw over masses of hot rocks, and so overcome her enemies. The lava surrounding the crater is blown by the wind out into fine strands, which the natives called "Pele's hair," and looked upon with reverence. Everybody stood in awe of Pele, and on her ground the "tabu" was more strictly kept than anywhere else.

About the year 1809 a sea-captain, stopping at the Sandwich Islands, found a boy about four-teen years of age whose name was Obookiah. His father and mother had been killed in one of the native wars, and as he was lonely and sad he gladly accepted the invitation of the captain to go back with him to America. The boy was ignorant, clumsy, and awkward, and had little about him that was bright or attractive in any way ; but the captain took him to his own home in Boston and did his best to make the young stranger happy. But Obookiah seemed not much more contented than when in his native land. The new country and the new life awoke new desires, and made him uneasy. One day he was found, by a man who was passing by, sitting on the steps of one of the buildings of Yale College crying as though his heart would break.

"What is the matter, my lad?" asked the stranger, pausing in surprise and sympathy. "Why are you weeping so distressingly?"

"Because there is n't anybody to teach me anything," whimpered the poor boy, rubbing his eyes to drive away the tears.

"Well," said the man, who had a kind heart and a generous spirit, "come along with me, and we'll see what we can do about it." And up jumped Obookiah, and followed his new friend with delight and confidence. He was placed in a Christian home and his education was begun at once. He studied with all his might, too, in order to make up for lost time. A while afterwards, Samuel Mills, who was one of the young men who had been present at the prayer-meeting held under the haystack in Williamstown, and who, like the others, had decided to be a missionary, fell in with Obookiah, and took him to his father's house in Torringford, Connecticut. There he learned many other things besides those lessons that were taught from books. A little later he wrote a letter to a friend in New Haven speaking of his advantages. He used to say "c-a-t pig," he wrote, but now he could spell in words of four syllables, and he now knew the "chief end of man," too. His first prayer was something like this: "Great and eternal God, make heaven, make earth, make everything, have mercy on me; make me understand the Bible; make me good; make me go back Owhyee, tell folks in Owhyee no more

pray to stone god; make some good man go with
me to Owhyee, tell folks in Owyhee about heaven. God, make all people good everywhere."

But Obookiah was only a boy, and often had
feelings that were not quite on a level with those
of his best moments. He owned afterwards that
at first he cared more about having religion in
his head than in his heart, and he made this
frank little confession besides: "Sometimes,"
he said, "when good people talked to me on this
subject, I was but just hate to hear it;" but he
did not stay long in this frame of mind, and soon
could say truthfully, "I cannot help think about
heaven. I go in a meadow, work at the hay
with my hands, but my heart no there: in heaven all the time. Then I feel very happy."

He was anxious to go back to his own land,
and tell his people about God and about Christ,
so he worked away at his studies with that end
in view. With the help of a friend he tried to
reduce his own language to writing, and he really did make what he called "a kind of spelling-
book, dictionary, and grammar."

Obookiah was himself one of the best proofs
that the church had ever had as to the value of
foreign missions. The dull look went out of his
face, which became bright and intelligent. His
awkwardness all disappeared, and his manners
became refined and graceful. In 1816 a school

was started in Cornwall, Connecticut, for the
purpose of educating other heathen boys, and
turning them into Christian gentlemen like
Henry Obookiah, but Obookiah himself never
carried the gospel to his countrymen, although
he fitted into God's plan for the salvation of
the Sandwich Islands just as truly as if he
had done as he hoped to do.   In 1819 he died.
"God will do right," he said.   " Let God do as
he pleases."

The school in Cornwall was given up in 1826,
as it was found wiser to educate the heathen in
their own countries, but Obookiah had pointed
out the missionary path to the Sandwich Islands,
and his wishes were not forgotten.   In 1820 two
students in the seminary at Andover, named
Hiram Bingham and Asa Thurston, decided to
devote themselves to this work, and with several
other volunteers they sailed for Hawaii.   The
way had been wonderfully prepared for them.

The king, Kamehameha, had become sovereign of all the islands, so they were now under
one government and for that reason would be
more easily reached.   Kamehameha had, besides, learned a little about the Christian religion from Captain Vancouver, who had visited
the islands several times, and the ideas of all
the people had changed in many points.   When
they saw that the sailors with whom they were

thrown could do without harm the things that they had never dared to they began to lose their faith in their system of "tabu," and to venture to break through its laws once in a while themselves. This disbelief grew all the time, and when Kamehameha was about to die he tried to gain more knowledge about the true God and his teachings from an American who was then at Hawaii; but this American was sadly ignorant on the subject himself and could do nothing to help the dying king. But after Kamehameha's death his wife, Kaahumanu, whose name means "The Feather Mantle," declared that there was no truth in the traditions about "tabu," and the whole system was swept from the island, except so far as the domains of Pele were concerned, who was as much an object of homage as ever. Kaahumanu also persuaded the people to throw away their idols, and before the missionaries landed they heard that the gods of stone, that Obookiah had prayed might be no longer worshipped, were indeed cast aside.

Captain Vancouver had led the natives to expect that men would come from England to teach them of a new religion, so they were not sure that these teachers from America would do as well. However the missionaries were at last allowed to come on shore; and were told that they might stay. They stationed themselves upon three of the largest islands, and began work by starting schools.

Kaahumanu was regent at that time, and at first she would have nothing to do with the missionaries; but in time she became interested in learning to read, and from the moment when she opened a book she threw aside her cards and her old amusements and devoted herself to study. Before long she was truly converted, and then she gave herself to the work of missions, using all her influence on the side of the teachers and doing all she could to help them. She opened schools in various places and herself travelled round the islands begging people to turn from their idols and to take up the new and better faith of the Christians.

Kapiolani was another important woman in Hawaii. She was the daughter of a chieftain and the wife of a man who was for a time governor of Hawaii. She was one of the first converts and she built a church at her home, near the spot where Captain Cook had been murdered. Before this time the meetings had been held under the open sky. As Kapiolani grew wiser in the lessons of the Bible she began to feel sure that the superstition about Pele was only a story, like all the other old tales, and she felt that it was time that it was outgrown. She

made up her mind to prove her belief by walking over the mountain and showing that she
could come back uninjured. Her friends to
whom she confided her intention begged her
not to be so rash as to risk her life in so dangerous an undertaking. Crowds of men and women
met her along the way and implored her to go
no further, but with her little New Testament
in her hand she pressed cheerily on. "If I am
destroyed you may all believe in Pele," she said.

A woman who claimed to be a prophetess
of the goddess stepped out upon the road and
warned Kapiolani not to go near the mountain
without an offering; but out came the Testament then, and reading her answers from that
the brave woman still kept on her course.

The people, though alarmed at her daring,
were really too curious in regard to her fate to
let her go out of their sight, so about eighty
persons, trembling with fear and excitement,
followed her towards the mountain. Straight
up its side she went and walked directly to the
brink of the crater, calmly nibbling some berries
that she had plucked along the path, which
were supposed to be sacred to Pele. Then she
carelessly flung stones into the opening, an
action that was said to be especially displeasing
to the being who dwelt in the burning volcano.
Still nothing unusual happened. The mass of

fire roared and swayed before the people, shooting flames thirty and forty feet into the air, while beneath their feet were loud explosions and the earth shook around them, but Kapiolani was not dismayed. "Jehovah is my God," she said, quietly. "He kindled these fires. I fear not Pele. Should I perish by her anger then you may fear her power; but if Jehovah save me when breaking her 'tabus' then must you fear and serve Jehovah. The gods of Hawaii are vain. Great is the goodness of Jehovah in sending missionaries to turn us from these vanities to the living God."

Then Kapiolani asked that a Christian hymn should be sung, and after a prayer was offered the people turned and went wonderingly home, and the power of Pele was broken forever.

Kapiolani was admired and honored all over the kingdom. A visitor to the islands said that she was so intelligent, so amiable, and so ladylike that nobody could meet her without feeling in her more than ordinary interest. When she spoke of what the missionaries had done for her country she said; "Our happiness is the joy of a captive just freed from prison;" but when she remembered the dreadful things that were once common in the islands she could not help thinking, "Oh, why didn't the missionaries come sooner?"

From this time the blessed work went rapidly on. Within ten years the language was reduced to a written form, parts of the Bible had been translated, and the printing-press at Honolulu was throwing off hundreds of pages of good reading matter. Churches were built, one of which held three thousand persons, and there were two hundred church members. In 1834 the first newspaper was published.

In 1835 the Rev. Titus Coan went to Hawaii and was stationed at Hilo, where about one-third of the people had learned to read and a church of thirty-six members had been formed. The first year he made circuit of the island by canoe and on foot, travelling over three hundred miles. He always spent a great deal of time in visiting, and he trained his native converts to go out two by two, on this sort of work, after the manner of the disciples long ago. They climbed mountains, went through forests, and crossed rivers, sometimes fording the streams, sometimes scrambling over, as well as they could, clinging to a rope fastened to the shore, to keep themselves from floating down with the rapid current.

After several of these tours interest began to waken all over the island and crowds flocked to Hilo to hear Mr. Coan preach. In 1837 there was a wonderful revival, and everybody, from

near and from far, came to listen to the message
of the gospel. Even sick people and old people
and lame people were brought on litters to the
services. Throngs gathered from all the villages,
and the natives put up shelters in which to live
while away from home. The cabins were thick
in every direction within a mile of the mission,
and the village of one thousand inhabitants
swelled suddenly to ten thousand. Meetings
were held every day and schools were opened for
the children. At any hour, by simply ringing a
bell, a congregation of six thousand might be
gathered in a moment. Those who became
Christians showed their earnestness by trying
to set right that which had been wrong in their
lives. Stolen things were given back, quarrels
were made up, lazy folk became industrious,
and drunkards stopped drinking. Within three
years over ten thousand converts were added to
the number of Christians.

A missionary who went to Hawaii in 1832 said
later that at his first service he had a congregation
of about twelve hundred natives, and a Sunday-
school of about seven hundred pupils. These people were almost all of them clothed in the native
cloth and seated on the ground. The meeting-
house was a large grass building, with open doors,
a rough pulpit and one window behind the pulpit.
In 1857 he kept his first jubilee. Then there was

a pretty church, and within its walls were gathered people from fifteen out-districts, all dressed in European style. In 1853 one-fourth of the population belonged to the various churches.

In 1862 the real mission work in Hawaii was over, because the Sandwich Islands were numbered among the Christian nations. In 1873 the connection of the islands with the American Board was severed, and the churches became independent of outside aid and control. Now sixty per cent. of the population will be found to be regular attendants at church, and Hawaii has a congregation numbering four thousand five hundred persons; one of the largest in the world.

So many foreigners have come to live in the islands that missions have to be carried on for their benefit. Among a population of ninety-thousand, fifty-five thousand people are from other lands. This fact, as well as that of the recent trouble between the rulers and the people and the still unsettled condition of the government, has done much to hinder the growth of true religion, and to arouse the old heathenism and wickedness; but the native Christian church holds on its way. Thirty per cent. of its ministers will be found to be missionaries and two per cent. of its missionary giving may be counted on for foreign countries. The Hawaiian children are early taught the art of giving. The mother will hold her baby's hand, with a penny in its grasp, over the contribution-box and gently shake it until the small fist uncloses and the money falls into the box. Then she kisses and pets the hand, and tries the plan again, until after a while the child learns to enjoy the performance, and thinks of giving as a pleasure.

It cost $1,250,000 to evangelize Hawaii, but during the fifty years of work in the islands that nation brought into our country $4,000,000 in trade.

General Armstrong, who was so long the head of the Industrial School at Hampton, Virginia, and who was the son of a missionary in Hawaii, has said: "What are Christians put into the world for except to do the impossible in the strength of God?"

What must have seemed to be impossible had in the strength of God been accomplished in the land from which General Armstrong came, and the beginning of the whole matter was so small a thing as the coming of a heathen boy to America so long ago.

One of the fields of the mission work of the converts of the Sandwich Islands is that group of which we have heard a little now and then as we have voyaged about the South Seas—the Marquesas Islands.

When the Duff had left the first missionaries at Tahiti, in 1797, it passed on and dropped
two teachers on these islands. The Marquesas
people were much like those on other cannibal
islands, only perhaps they were more wicked
and cruel and more elaborately tattooed than
many other tribes in the Pacific. They were
marked with figures of fishes, lizards and stars,
and they had besides added to the beauty of
their decorations by rubbing themselves with
oil, day after day, until some of the older ones
had taken on a polish like that on old furniture,
and beneath this covering the lines of the tattooing might be traced as veins and marks may
be seen in wood.

They were also given to the use of ornaments made of teeth and shells and feathers,
and some of them wore long white cloaks that
fell from their shoulders to their heels. The
other garments were skirts and some sort of
waists formed of scarfs flowing across the chest.
Their cloth is made from the inner bark of
trees, softened in water and pounded by a mal-
let into a soft white material.

The natives are divided into almost number-
less clans, and are always at war among themselves. The first teachers did not stay long
with them, but in 1825 some others came to
them and tried to settle in the islands, but the

natives threatened to kill and to eat them if they did not take themselves speedily away, so the men returned to Tahiti. In 1832 three American missionaries, among whom were the father and mother of General Armstrong, had a similar experience, and the mission was given up altogether for a while.

But in 1853 some result of all this seed-sowing began to appear. A chief of one of the islands put to sea in a whale-ship and came, over one thousand miles, to the Sandwich Islands to ask that a missionary might be sent to him and his friends. "We have nothing but war, war, war," he said; "and fear, trouble and poverty. We are tired of living so, and wish to be as you are here."

The churches were much interested in this man and his errand, and the people contributed willingly to the expense of fitting out an expedition to the Marquesas Islands. On the sixteenth of June two native pastors and two deacons, with their wives, sailed for the Marquesas in a brig chartered for the purpose at a cost of $2,000. They were accompanied by a white missionary, who would help them in starting their work and then come home.

They were joyfully greeted by the natives, but the French were jealous of this intrusion into what they called their territory, and commanded the chiefs to send away the teachers. The chiefs, however, refused to obey, and the Protestant missionaries were soon established in a house owned by one of the tribes, and the work has been carried on in spite of the opposition of the French and the Romanists, and through many difficulties of all kinds. The native teachers have proved themselves capable and faithful, and have won honor outside of their place of labor as well as within it.

Peruvian pirates had carried away so many of the people for slaves that the savage chief of one clan vowed that he would kill and eat the first white man that fell in his way. This man happened to be the mate of an American whaler; but he was saved from the horrible death designed for him by the gallantry of Kekela, one of the Hawaiian teachers, who rescued him by offering the natives, in exchange for their victim, a six-oared boat just received from Boston.

Abraham Lincoln heard of this action, and sent Kekela a valuable present in token of the gratitude of the United States. In his note of reply Kekela said : " As to this friendly deed of mine, its seed was brought from your own land by some of your own people who had received the love of God. It was planted in Hawaii, and I brought it here that these dark regions might

receive the root of all which is good and true,
and that is all. How shall I repay your great
kindness? This is my only payment—that which
I have read of the Lord—love."

Could anything have been more modestly
and more gracefully expressed?

The great need now among these people is
an increase of missionaries; but that spirit of
love that reigns in the hearts of those already in
the field will surely conquer at last, even in the
dark regions of the Marquesas.

CHAPTER XIII.

MICRONESIA : THE "LITTLE ISLANDS."

THE word Micronesia means "The Little Islands." The clusters that bear this name lie in the Pacific Ocean southwest of Hawaii. The principal groups that make up this division are the Caroline, Gilbert or Kingswell, Marshall and Ladrone Islands; but there are many smaller circles that come under this title, too.

Most of these islands are low and barren, with a lagoon in the centre. They rest like green rings on the surface of the ocean, having no hills nor streams, few land birds, and no flowers. No horses, cows nor sheep can live on them long, and on one island, that of Apaiang, the soil is so poor that only twenty-five kinds of growing things can be found there, including every sort of shrub and weed. Some of the islands, however, like Ponape and Kusaie, are volcanic, and have mountains two or three thousand feet high. They are also covered with forests which are filled with the songs of birds of gay plumage, that make the woods brilliant with color. The trees are the bread-fruit, banana, cocoanut, lemon and orange, with a great variety of timber trees.   The people build little reed houses under them and plant round them bananas and yams, training the vines of the latter plant upon the trees.

The people of Micronesia are of two kinds. Some are copper-colored and some are olive in hue.   They have black eyes and straight black hair, and when they were first known by white men many of them were frightfully tattooed. Their dress was different in the different islands. In the Marshall group the costume was made up of two mats braided by hand from the leaves of the pandanus tree, with an edge embroidered with bark dyed brown, black or yellow, and put in in all sorts of ingenious patterns.   These were worn tied round the waist by a cord, and with the man the skirt was made to stand out before and behind in a remarkable manner.   The men arranged their hair on the top of the head, and all the natives had their ears pierced early in life, and then, by taking first small sticks and then larger ones and forcing them through the opening, the hole was gradually enlarged until, in some cases, a man's arm might be thrust through without touching the flesh.   A fashionable young man might sometimes have been seen with an enormous cup fastened in each ear. In the Caroline Islands the men wore cocoanut trousers and a skirt of deep fringe.   This style of skirt was also worn by the women. The men were fond of trinkets, and adorned themselves with many kinds of ornaments, from wreaths to belts and necklaces. As they had no pockets they carried their pipes in their ears. The people of the Gilbert Islands had little clothing of any sort.

The natives of these islands are as much at home in the water as on the land, and they dive to great depths. A favorite pastime with the boys is to bend a tall, slender sapling over the water in such a way that when they have climbed to its tip they will be flung out into the waves. They also find great amusement on surf-boards, with which they ride over the waves to the shore with ease and delight.

The islanders had no meat nor milk, and their food was largely obtained from the cocoanut-tree. They got something like milk from the grated meat of the nut and this was used in many ways in preparing their meals. The sap from the bud makes a pleasant drink, and when boiled makes a good syrup. If allowed to ferment it supplies yeast for bread. The water of the young cocoanut is also helpful in quenching thirst. When the meat of the nut is ripe it is dried and sold as food, and thus it serves the natives as money with which to buy articles that they need. They also eat the fruit of the pandanus tree, which, when cooked, is almost as good as pumpkin. It is dried and kept for long voyages or for hard times. Dishes and bottles for holding water, oil and sap were formed from the cocoanut shells, and now from the fibre of the husk are manufactured cords, ropes, scrubbing-brushes and door-mats. The cocoa palm gives them also timber for building and for making spears, as well as oil, and material for torches, fuel and medicine. It grows in great luxuriance on these islands. The fruit has a peculiar shape that keeps it afloat after it has fallen into the water, so that it is carried all over the South Seas and plants its seeds on many shores. The bread-fruit also is a valuable tree, and is of great service in the making of canoes, some of which are fifty or sixty feet long. They are ingeniously put together, and the men are skilful navigators. They steer without chart or compass, and are guided by the moon, the stars and the wave-lines.

The leaves of the pandanus are as useful as the fruit, although in a different way. From these leaves are made mats, sails, hats, and such things, and the trunk furnishes strong and hard timber.

The inhabitants of these islands were once all wicked and ignorant and hard-hearted. They were thieves and liars, and were cruel to women and to old people. They believed in spirits, and brought offerings to stones set up in their honor. Their only occupations were fishing and fighting.

It was to these islands that there came in the year 1852 three American missionaries, sent by the American Board, bringing with them their wives and two native teachers from the Sandwich Islands. They settled upon the Caroline group and there worked for five years without much encouragement. Then the boat called the Morning Star was built by money given by the Sunday-school children of the United States, and this ship went out to Micronesia bearing three new missionaries, among whom was Hiram Bingham, the son of the man of the same name who had gone to Hawaii in 1819.

The missionaries scattered their forces among the three larger groups, and Ebon in the Marshall Islands, Ponape and Kusaie in the Caroline Islands and Apaiang in the Gilbert Islands were occupied by mission families. Hiram Bingham and his wife set up a station at Apaiang; that place in which but twenty-five kinds of things would grow, and where there were still fewer signs of any of the fruits of the Spirit among the natives.

Hiram Bingham had taken with him material for a cottage, and he at once put up his little house on some land given him by the king. Then he and his wife began to learn the language and tried to give it a written form, and they were very glad when a small printing-press was sent to them. Here, however, they met fresh difficulties, for the types had been chosen with respect to the English language, and there were too many d's and h's for the Gilbert tongue, and not enough r's and k's. But Mr. Bingham was clever and ingenious. He mastered the trouble by cutting off the tops of the small d's and turning them into r's, and by making a notch in the little h's and transforming them into k's. He did not know much about printing, either, but was seeking first the kingdom of God and this thing that he needed was added unto him. Just about this time an expert printer was wrecked near this island and he came over to Apaiang, hoping to catch the Morning Star before she should start on her homeward trip. But she had left the place two days before his arrival, and so he was laid hold upon by the good missionary, and had the honor of directing the first printing ever done in the Gilbert language.

During the nine following years there was steady progress in the work at all the mission stations, in spite of the disheartening beginning in Micronesia. Three churches were started, and there was teaching, preaching and translation going on all the time, and the churches grew rapidly. After ten years of voyaging among the islands the Morning Star was sold because she was becoming old and decrepit; but in 1856 Mr. and Mrs. Bingham went home, and Mr. Bingham raised enough money to build another one, and as he had been studying navigation meanwhile he set out the next year as captain of the second Morning Star and sailed around the Horn for the third time. He was in command of the vessel for a year and a half, and journeyed back and forth from Honolulu to Apaiang. This vessel, too, gave way to another of the same name, as she was wrecked in the year 1859.

For various reasons there was at this time but one white missionary in Micronesia. This was the Rev. E. T. Doane; but in 1871 the third Morning Star brought back some of the former missionaries and some new native teachers from Hawaii for the Gilbert Islands. In 1873 the Morning Star carried native missionaries from Ponape to the Mortlock Islands. Among these teachers was the Princess Opatinia, the daughter of King Hezekiah, the chief of the island, with her husband Opataia. They went forth most joyfully upon their errand of love, willingly giving up all the comforts and honors and enjoyments of their homes for the sake of their needy neighbors. Their letters were eagerly waited for in the church at Ponape and read to attentive crowds, ready to weep or rejoice with those who wept or rejoiced on the new field. In less than five years the brave pioneers had established on the Mortlock Islands seven churches, with three hundred and thirty-eight members altogether. The natives were devoted to these kind friends, built houses for them, brought them food, denying themselves in time of famine so that their teachers should not suffer want, and did all their work in order that they might have more leisure for studying and preaching.

Help was next given to the island of Pingelap. Six natives of this island had been brought by a trader to Ponape as servants. When their time of service ended he set them adrift, and in their helpless condition they fell in with a missionary, who let them use some native houses and have a little land to cultivate. He also took them into school, where they became so deeply interested that they would often sit up until midnight to study by the light of a cocoanut-oil lamp. They became Christians, and two of them were baptized, under the names of Thomas and David, and then went back to Pingelap with the story of the gospel. At first they met a good deal of opposition from their own people,

and an old priest gathered a large crowd of
natives and told them that he would prove to
them that this religion was false by killing the
teachers by his incantations. But instead of
having his charms work as he had planned he
himself fell down insensible, and the prayers
of the two whom he had meant to destroy
were followed by his restoration. The people
declared that the new faith had conquered, and
all went over to that side. A new teacher came
from Ponape, and in place of the queer houses,
that were only thatched roofs resting on the
ground, with a hole in the gable through which
the occupants scrambled in and out, there was
soon a village of good dwellings with proper
doors and windows, and a fine church that would
hold six hundred persons. One of the two teachers who had been first in Pingelap became the
pastor, and this little church, besides taking care
of itself, has sent about $100 every year to the
American Board for its missionary fund.

In 1874 Mr. Taylor, Mr. Logan and Mr. Rand
joined the missionary ranks in Micronesia, and
in 1875 Hiram Bingham and his wife went to
Honolulu to devote themselves to the translation of the Bible into the Gilbert language. In
all parts of the mission more attention was now
paid to building up training-schools and educating native teachers.

When the missionaries began work at Ponape there were some people there from the
Gilbert Islands, among whom were a man and a
woman with their child, a boy baby.   These
people fell into a quarrel with the natives, and
the father and mother of the boy were killed in
battle.   After the fight was over the poor little
fellow was picked up from the ground by a woman of rank, who hid him from his enemies for
a while and then gave him over to the care of
one of the missionaries.   He became a Christian,
as he grew older, and thinking that his story
was something like that of Moses he was baptized under the name of the grand old leader of
the Israelites.   Then he wished to start out as
a missionary.   So he was sent over to the Mortlock group, where he stayed two years, gathering a church of eighty-six members.   Then he
moved on, to another island, and founded a
church of fifty-seven members.

In 1879 he went to the island of Ruk, where
there were about ten thousand people sunk in
darkness and crime; but one year brought a
wondrous change to the inhabitants.   When
the Morning Star stopped at Ruk after a twelve
months' absence she was welcomed by a crowd
of children clapping their hands and singing
Sunday-school songs.   They led the visitors that
had come on the ship up a pleasant path to the

spot where the teacher's home was nestled under
the trees, and pointed to the new church building not far away.   After that time, whenever
the Morning Star called at this island, she
found that the mission begun by Moses at Ruk
was stepping along at a steady pace.

A native teacher had been placed at Ape-
mama too.   This was one of the Gilbert Islands,
and was in no better condition in many ways
than that other island of Ruk.   In a short time
he had gathered about one hundred pupils into
his school, but he did not find them always easy
to manage.   The king was jealous of any one
who, he feared, knew more than himself, and
if any of his school-mates went above him in
the class he would at once order his head to
be cut off, that he himself might always be first.
But the work went on, and the king learned
more justice and self - control, and cleverness
was not quite so dangerous a trait as it had
been.   After seven or eight years a church of
seventy-one members was formed, and in ten
years there were about three hundred persons
wishing to be added to the roll.

About the year 1882 twelve natives of this
island left home for a short voyage over to another group, but being overtaken by a storm
they were driven far out of their course, and
from October to December their vessel was

beating about in the ocean, unable to make any harbor. At last those who survived were discovered, by the Northern Light. about six hundred miles distant from their native land. All the food that remained to them was a small quantity of dried pulverized banana, and a few bottles of cocoanut-oil. They had also about six gallons of water.

Perhaps the sailors on the Northern Light were a little afraid to take in these people from a savage island, for experience would have taught them that the natives whom they met in the waters of the Pacific were often not the most safe and pleasant companions in the world, but, to their surprise, these wanderers seemed to be devout Christians.

No sooner were they on board the ship than one of them offered thanks to the One who had rescued them from their perilous position, and then they all hastened to express their gratitude to these earthly friends who had held out to them a helping hand.

Owing to the unfavorable currents, they could not be landed upon their own shores, but they were taken to Yokohama, in Japan, where the foreign residents were so much pleased with their looks and their behavior that they raised a sum of money for the purpose of helping them to find their way home.

The Morning Star went on its voyages year after year, bearing missionaries and messages and goods back and forth over the water, and carrying converts from one island to another as bringers of good tidings. As the little messenger with its white wings would approach the shore of some unknown island the natives would run away and hide themselves in the woods. Gradually growing a little bolder they would peep out from behind the trees, and perhaps a few of their bravest warriors would venture to risk themselves in a canoe and steal out towards the strange ship, from which would be sent to meet them a native from another island, so that they need not be alarmed at sight of a being too unlike themselves. This native would tell them as well as he could, considering the difference in dialect between various islands, that there were other countries in the world besides their own, and that the people from these countries knew many marvellous things of which the poor islanders had never heard, and that they were willing to leave with them a man who would tell them about all these wonders, and would teach them a great deal, and help them in many ways. If the natives agreed to the plan some teachers were set upon the shore and the ship would sail away, leaving the missionaries and their families to their task.

For a whole year nothing is heard from them and they know nothing of the outside world. But when the time draws near for the appearance of the Morning Star on its annual visit how eagerly and longingly beat the hearts of these lonely teachers as they wait for the cry of "Sail-ho!" from some watcher in a tree-top or down on the beach. Ah, there it is at last: "Sail-ho!" The cry is taken up by one voice and another until the sound goes ringing through the trees. The flag of the pretty vessel is run up in the breeze, and the salute is answered by hats and handkerchiefs, as well as by branches waved in the air. A boat is launched from the shore, and then comes the joyful meeting. It is only to be appreciated by those who have been exiled so long from home and friends. There is much to tell and hear about on both sides, and how happy are the men on the Morning Star when they can bring to these thirsty souls good news from a far country, and can take back pleasant tidings of peace and prosperity in the mission work of the island. Sometimes, too, there would be cheering hints of awakening from neighboring islands, the natives of whom had sent word to the missionaries near them, "Give us teachers, too, that we may learn the good way, and stop fighting."

After thirteen years of labor this Morning

Star, too, was tumbled upon the beach and broken to pieces in a storm. The Micronesians felt very sad over this mishap. " Me, too, much sorry Morning Star broke," said one of them. " No come back to us any more."

A barkentine with steam attachment was next given to this work in the Pacific, and it made its first voyage in 1884. The figure-head was the figure of a woman holding an open Bible in her hand.

Within the last ten years there has been a steady increase in the number of converts and of hearers in these islands of Micronesia. In 1885 the Germans took possession of the Marshall Islands and tried to seize the Carolines too, but the Spanish nation stepped up just then, and would not allow Spain's claim to be set aside. The mission work in the islands had never been in a more hopeful state than at this time. Many of the chiefs had been baptized, and the evil of kava-drinking had been nearly rooted out of Ponape. The missionaries were sorry that the native independence was not respected and the chiefs assisted in forming a government that would have been advantageous on all sides, but the Spanish established themselves in Ponape and did their best to interfere with the work of the missions. Schools were closed, and the chiefs influenced to hinder preaching and the building of churches, and the cultivation of the kava-plant was encouraged. The intruders laid hold of lands deeded to missionaries, and when Mr. Doane objected to this sort of robbery he was arrested and imprisoned; but he was soon set at liberty by the governor-general at Manilla, who spoke warmly of the services of the missionaries to the islands, and paid high tribute to their characters. Soon afterwards a new governor was sent to Ponape, who promised protection to both the missionaries and the natives.

In 1891, however, the Spaniards began to make trouble again, and Mr. Rand, who was at work in Ponape, was driven away, with his fellow-laborers, and was obliged to take refuge in a neighboring island. They work as well as they can from their present post, and a fine young native named Henry Naupei, an assistant in the training-school in Ponape, does wonderfully well in their place. He preaches and teaches, and makes tours round the island cheering the Christians, and helping them to stand fast in the faith in spite of all opposition. Sometimes the missionaries call at the island, and the young teacher comes out to their ship and a little conference is held on board. He has recently written a letter saying that the native Christians mean to spread the work just as far as they are able. The German rule is very oppressive on the Marshall Islands.

On the Gilbert Islands, Hiram Bingham has lived to see eleven churches on thirteen islands, and to rejoice in sixteen hundred Christians among those whom he found savages. In the spring of 1893, after thirty-four years of toil, Mr. Bingham had the pleasure of standing in the pressroom of the American Bible Society in New York and reading aloud the last verse in the proof of his completed translation of the Bible in the Gilbert language. He then saw the last type set, and watched the first revolution of the roller that would so far help to send his book out in completed form. The whole Bible was printed on that day, and in the afternoon several volumes were bound and given as souvenirs to persons who were present. This translation will open the Bible to about twenty thousand people. Hiram Bingham is, so far as is known, the only man who ever reduced a language to writing, made a vocabulary and a grammar, translated the whole Bible into that language, revised all the proofs, and finally held the finished book in his hand. He has now gone back to distribute his precious volumes among the waiting islanders. A new boat, called the Hiram Bingham, has recently been built for the benefit of the Gilbert Islands.

The population of Micronesia is about eighty-four thousand. There are forty-six self-supporting churches and forty-three hundred members. About fifty - thousand people have heard the gospel. This work has been done in about forty years. A strong missionary spirit is seen in the churches in Micronesia. It has been reported that the king of the Gilbert group has been making a missionary tour through his kingdom. That the people are eager to learn is shown by this list of books in their own language carried them in one cargo, by the Morning Star: 750 arithmetics, 250 geographies, 750 readers, 750 hymn-books, 465 New Testaments, and 205 books of Bible stories.

Last year the American Board called for more workers for Micronesia. A man is needed in the Ruk lagoon, where Robert Logan has lately died of fever. Robert Logan fought in the civil war in the United States, and then went out to fight the Lord's battle in Micronesia, where, like a brave soldier, he fell on the field, faithful to the last. He was greatly loved and admired both by the missionaries and the natives. The field is white unto the harvest. Let us pray that the Lord of the harvest will send out laborers to gather it in.

CHAPTER XIV.

THE LAND OF THE "CRISP-HAIRED."

NEW GUINEA, or Papua, is said to be the largest island in the world, now that Australia is counted as a continent. It was discovered in the sixteenth century by the Portuguese, and was called by them New Guinea, because they thought that it looked like Guinea in Africa. The native name, Papua, means "crisp-haired."

New Guinea is about fourteen hundred miles long, and is about four hundred miles wide in some places. It is a mountainous island covered with forests. In the interior are some very high mountains. There are also many swamps, and the climate is warm and moist. There is a great deal of fever along the coast, and on the whole the country is not a healthful one in which to live.

But there are in New Guinea some rare and wonderful things that make up for some of the drawbacks. There are many beautiful kinds of birds, from parrots and cockatoos to the bird of paradise and the cassowary, and there are numerous sorts of insects. One traveller collected one thousand species of beetle in one square mile, in

three months' time. One of the most remarkable birds is the megapodius, which is about the
size of a large fowl, with an egg three and a half
inches in length and two inches in diameter. It
buries its eggs in high mounds built of sand,
loose earth, sticks, leaves, and stones, and leaves
them to be hatched by the sun.

The population of New Guinea is nearly one
million. There are two races of people on the
island, but the real Papuan is of brown complex-
ion with black hair. There are many different
languages or dialects spoken in Papua.

The inhabitants of the northern and western
parts, having come more frequently into contact
with other people, are more civilized than the
rest of the natives, and have some good towns
with fine streets and comfortable houses, where
live the traders, planters, and fishermen ; but
farther inland everything is nearer to a savage
state.   The people live in villages in which the
houses have thatched roofs and the sides are
covered with cocoanut leaves.   Some of these
villages are built over swamps, where the
streets are laid with large trees, and the houses
are raised on poles fifteen feet high and are
reached by ladders.   In front of these lofty
dwellings are elevated platforms, each one of
which is enclosed with a fence that bounds a
gay garden bed blooming with tropical plants

and flowers. One house is often three hundred feet long, and will hold all the people of the village. Many of these homes are lighted by the burning of the shells of the young cocoanut, and a string of shells is not seldom seen hanging above a fireplace.

Long platforms slope up to the temples, or *dubus*, as they are called, and there are bridges here and there across the creeks. The temples are large, and are divided into courts on each side of a long aisle, with the sacred place at one end. The partitions of the courts are formed of cocoanut leaves reaching to about nine feet from the floor, while curtains of sago-palm fronds hang from the roofs to the tops of these lower screens. Inside the courts are skulls of men, women, and children, crocodiles, and wild boars, some of them carved and colored. There is usually a fireplace, too. Within the inner sanctuary are often found queer figures carved out of cane. They look like fishes, with mouths like frogs, and they have bodies about nine feet long and seven broad.

Some houses are built directly over the water, and sometimes the baby of the family will fall through a crack in the bamboo floor into the stream below, but as the nurses all know how to swim he is easily rescued.

Other villages are on rich land, and are sur-

rounded by cocoanut-palms. Some houses are
perched in trees, with ladders for stairways.
Altogether, one wishing to settle in New Guinea
would have a wide choice in regard to the manner of housekeeping he would adopt.

In the interior of the island the people wear
little clothing. In some places the women have
petticoats of palm-leaves dyed in various colors,
and both men and women tattoo and paint
themselves and delight in decorations of all
sorts. In some tribes the hair is arranged in
two great mops, one on each side of the head;
in others the heads are cropped in odd patterns,
square, circular, or triangular in shape. For
further ornamentation, when they are in full
dress some of the natives adorn themselves with
plumes of the young palm-fronds, which are fastened to their backs and wave gracefully over
their heads, while colored leaves are hung from
their arms, wrists and legs.

The natives about Port Moresby, on the
southern coast, believe that one of their ancestors made the earth, the sea and the sky, and
the ancestor of another line of chiefs made man.
They believe, too, in a god of fate, who deals
good and evil, success and failure, as he may
please. A number of villages are named after
this god, and in the planting-season a priest has
to go through certain ceremonies in order that

he may be persuaded to grant good crops. If a man have a good soul good comes to him, if evil himself he can expect nothing but evil. The soul is called Tirava, and when it leaves the body it is supposed to travel to a land far away towards the setting sun beyond Cape Suckling, the last bold promontory to the west. There the sago-palm grows in abundance, and anyone who enters this delightful place may eat as much sago as he may wish. Some tribes believe in a being whom they call the Maker, and some of them say that he once came to earth as a man. They think that good men after death go to live in the Milky Way, where there are groves filled with fruit, and joys of every kind abound.

When anyone dies the relatives blacken their faces and cover themselves with ashes, to show their grief. The women are devoted to their children, and mourn unceasingly when a little one is taken away, and as they have no hope of ever meeting a friend again in a better world they cling fondly to what is left to them. One poor woman had all the bones of a dead child strung into a necklace, which she wore as a token of love and faithfulness.

The people have an idea that in sleep the spirit deserts the body and wanders out to meet other spirits, who whisper to it warnings or promises of what will take place in the future.

For this reason they have great faith in dreams, and order their actions according to what they learn in this manner. If on a journey they pass a spot where anybody has died they strike their feet with a stick, as a charm to ward off an attack of the spirit that is hovering near and may try to stop their progress. The feathers of the cassowary are sometimes waved in the air for the same purpose. There are men who pretend to call up any kind of weather that may seem to them desirable by conjuring with some small wooden figures, which they have named the makers of heaven and earth, thunder and lightning, southeast and north-west winds. These figures are placed side by side, and an object shaped like a sort of shuttle-cock is held up near them when thunder is to be summoned or driven away. When wind is desired the figures are placed in the direction from which it is invited to come and the shuttle-cock is differently handled.

One of the favorite occupations of the men of New Guinea is fishing for dugong. The dugong is a fish that is ten feet long and has a mouth like a horse, a head like a pig and a body like a porpoise. A sharp, jagged iron bolt is used in spearing this fish. The spear shaft is fifteen feet long, and ends in a round, heavy knob for the purpose of carrying the weapon home. The flesh of the dugong makes excellent food.

When fresh it tastes like beef or veal, and when cured like bacon. It is caught at the new and the full of the moon, when the high tides cover the reefs. Another amusement is hunting kan- garoos, which the Papuans call wallabies.

The natives are very expert at carving. In some tribes the men accomplish wonders with a nail, a shell, or a piece of sharp flint. They also make pottery, which they barter for cocoanuts and sago with other tribes, going on long voy- ages to the Gulf of New Guinea for the sake of disposing of their wares. For these trips they build queer sort of craft called lakatois. They tie several canoes together and upon them place a firm platform of poles upon which a deck is laid, and strong houses are put up fore and aft. Often new canoes are made on the way, and these are added to the vessels, sometimes making them so unwieldy that one or two have to be allowed to drift away. The sail of a laka- toi is formed from mats and shaped like a large shield, or the biggest claw of a crab. When their destination is reached the men arrange the pot- tery in a row on the beach and two sticks of wood are placed in each piece, one stick being taken by the buyer, the other by the seller. When the lakatoi is about to leave the village the wood is brought out and the visitors are given a bundle of sago for each stick that they hold.

Among the religious ceremonies of New Guinea is a dance connected with one of their sacred feasts. The men who are to take part in the performance are called Kaevakuku, and they leave their homes and do not see their families for at least three moons before the festival. At the proper time, they adorn themselves with masks, from two to four feet high, like a fool's cap with an animal's face. The dress varies with the tribe. In some of the tribes a cloak two and a half feet long is worn, and a kilt about eighteen inches long, both made from the fibre of the yellow hibiscus. Some of the men look like walking haystacks. Food is piled up on the platforms in front of the temples, and is also hung round on poles. The actors come out of the bush in their costumes and masks, singly or in groups, and dance about until food is given to them, when they go back again. The masks are all burned in one big bonfire at the close of the ceremony.

The custom of buying wives is not as common in New Guinea as in many savage nations, but some tribes do pay for this sort of a blessing. One chief boasted proudly that his wife had cost him ten arm-shells, three pearl shells, two strings of dogs' teeth, several hundreds of cocoanuts, a large number of yams, and two pigs.

Mission work in New Guinea was begun in

1854 by the Dutch missionaries. They were
all laid low by fever, again and again, but they
held on as long as they could, until at the close
of five years every one died. The Utrecht Missionary Society sent out others to take their
places, and these men translated part of the
New Testament into one of the native dialects;
but though they started churches and schools,
and accomplished good in several ways, there
were not half enough workers for all that there
was to be done. About 1872 the London Missionary Society came to the help of the laborers
in New Guinea. Mr. Murray, Mr. MacFarlane,
and Mr. Gill stepped over from their fields in
the islands of Polynesia to plunge into toil in
Papua. They took with them converts from
the Samoan, Loyalty and Savage Islands, and
left them to fight their own way as strangers in
a strange land. Twelve were killed, but their
places were instantly filled by willing recruits,
and in 1877 James Chalmers, who had been for
ten years in Rarotonga, changed his post for one
in New Guinea. The headquarters of the New
Guinea Mission were about that time removed
to Murray Island. The eastern part of the mission was under the care of the Rev. W. G.
Lawes and the stations in the western portion
of the Gulf of New Guinea were watched over
by the Rev. S. Macfarlane. There were be-

sides fifteen Polynesian teachers, and ten more
went with Mr. Chalmers and Mr. Macfarlane
to plant missions at the eastern end of the pen-
insula.   They found a place that suited them
for a station on Stacey's Island, not far from
the main land.   The natives were friendly, and
gave the newcomers half of the largest house
in the village to live in while they were building a home for themselves, in a pleasant spot
in a grove of bread-fruit trees.   In 1878 Mr.
Chalmers had to leave his wife at the station
while he went to Cooktown for stores.   He was
a little afraid to have her stay there without
him, but she said bravely, "We came here for
Christ's sake, and he will protect us."   She was
ill while he was away, but by her tact and kindness she won the hearts of the people, and
gained a good deal of influence over them.

CHAPTER XV.

"GOD'S MEN" IN NEW GUINEA.

AFTER Mr. Chalmers returned to his station he undertook a sort of Robinson Crusoe tour of the island with the object of searching out the most healthful parts and choosing places where missions might be begun.

He made many friends on these journeys, and opened the way for future work. Then the mission steamer Ellengowan took him along the coast on a visit to one hundred and five villages, in ninety of which the inhabitants had never before seen the face of a white man. They must have looked at this one with great curiosity and interest, and probably thought him much too pale for beauty. At one place he had a narrow escape with his life but was saved by the interference of a friendly chief. He learned afterwards that the people of that village made a point of killing all strangers.

About this time Mrs. Chalmers became so feeble that she was obliged to go to Sydney, in Australia, and poor Mr. Chalmers had to work along by himself, without her help, companionship or sympathy. But he did not give himself up to moping or mourning, but occupied himself in the pleasant task of translating hymns. "We can reach the people sooner by singing the gospel than by preaching it," he said.

Later in the year the John Williams came along bringing more teachers from Polynesia. Eight of these men were from the Loyalty group. As they drew near the shore somebody began to talk about the dangers and the disagreeable things that awaited them in the shape of climate, centipedes, serpents and insects.

"Hold," said one of the Loyalty volunteers; "are there men there?"

"Men? yes; but they are horrible cannibals. They will probably kill and eat us in the twinkling of an eye."

"Never mind," returned the other man; "that settles it. Wherever there are men, there are missionaries bound to go." So on they sailed.

In 1879 Mrs. Chalmers grew rapidly worse and finally died in Sydney. Mr. Chalmers had started to go to her, and only learned of her death by picking up a newspaper while on his journey and reading there the notice that told him that he should never see her again in this world.

After the death of his wife Mr. Chalmers

moved to Port Moresby and made that town
his central station. In 1880 he decided to devote six weeks to exploring the country behind the mountains called the "Owen Stanley
Range." He made up a party and sent on ahead,
by some natives going in that direction, a large
supply of food, and articles for barter, keeping
only enough of both kinds of things for the
western part of the trip, which would take six
months of hard walking. He could find few
carriers, so he and his friends had to trudge
along under the burning sun laden with their
own burdens. It is this difficulty of carrying
that has prevented much exploration in New
Guinea.

The country was very rough. Often the trav-
ellers had to wade for hours in a stream and they
scrambled through many mountain torrents.
At last they reached a village built on the top of
a large table-rock and surrounded by a high bar-
ricade. They encamped for the night on the
side of a hill at the foot of which flowed a river.
In the morning they put a raft together to carry
them down this river, but before long they were
upset and had to crawl out of the water to the
shore, where they built large bonfires with
which to warm and dry themselves. The next
day they hired a canoe at a village and sailed
twenty miles, to the home of one of the teachers.

Altogether they had passed over five hundred miles and climbed forty thousand feet.

Mr. Chalmers' next expedition led him along the coast towards the west, where he preached in some places and gained a good many new acquaintances among the natives. In 1881 the church at Port Moresby was opened and the first three converts were baptized. The natives called Mr. Chalmers "Tamate," which means teacher, and they had great confidence in him. He heard, in some way, that some savage chiefs from the western part of the island were forming plans to fall upon the mission station, kill Mr. Chalmers and the teachers, and then attack the natives. These chiefs were a terror all along the shore and were a great hindrance to the work of the missionaries, so Mr. Chalmers made up his mind to go to meet these wild warriors on their own ground and see what he could do with them. Some of the natives were afraid to go with him on so dangerous an errand, but one of the baptized converts and several other men were glad to accompany him. "It's all right," they said, "if we go with Tamate. We'll soon be back with sago and betel-nuts; or, anyway, if Tamate lives we shall live, and if he is murdered we shall be murdered, too. We will go with Tamate."

All along the way the friendly natives tried

to stop the party by warnings, and by promises
of presents if these rash adventurers would but
turn back.   But nothing could persuade Tamate
and his followers to give up the expedition, as
the safety of the mission was at stake.

At last the village of the robber chieftains
was reached and the men were invited to engage in a sort of conference.   They agreed to
the plan, and Tamate beguiled them into making peace and obtained from them a promise
that they would not molest their neighbors.
Mr. Chalmers held a service for them besides.
To be sure, they ran away as fast as they could
go when he began to pray, but they were lured
back by the singing, and they listened attentive-
ly to his words and to those of a brother chief
who had come with him.

Not long afterwards Mr. Chalmers made another effort to spread his mission a little farther
westward, and in spite of wars and disturbances
among the various tribes he managed, by his
grace of manner and his skill and tact with the
natives, to keep them from destroying one another and to draw them into the work of starting stations.   At one place, where everything
was just ready to boil over into a deadly fight, he
stepped in, smoothed over the trouble, calmed
both sides and brought back good feeling.   One
of the men who had gone with him said, admir-

ingly : " As the sun shines, so do you. Such a
thing as you have now done has never before
been done on this coast, and it is only by the
gospel of peace that it could be done." Then
all the crew joined in, as a sort of chorus, with
" True, true, very true."

They had a very good name for the missionaries, these simple-hearted natives. They called
them " God's men."

On Mr. Chalmers' next journey westward he
found some of the men from Port Moresby on
a trading voyage to the village of the robber
chieftains. They told him that they had not
forgotten their training at the mission, though
they were so far from home. They always asked
God's blessing upon their food, and held services
morning and evening. One of the men had a
bell, which he rang around the village to tell the
people of the meetings, and many of them had
come in to share in the service. The converts
had kept Sunday in mind by tying every day
a knot in a cord ; when they had counted as far
as seven they would stop work for a day of
rest.

In 1883 Mr. Chalmers joined a party going
to the Gulf of Guinea in a lakatoi on a trading
voyage. From the coast he walked inland to
one of the villages over the swamps, where the
people had heard of him and asked for a visit.

He was kindly received, and put in one of the temples to sleep among the carved skulls and other objects that were pleasant reminders that he was among cannibals. In the evening he sat out on the balcony and watched the scene about him. The dark temple was lighted by the flickering firelight within, while below him a crowd of savages was gathered around the teachers, among whom was that man who had been one of the first church members at Port Moresby, and another man who had been a fierce and warlike chief. The teachers were telling of the love of Jesus Christ, and the savages were listening with great interest. They had, indeed, so many questions to ask at the close of the little sermon that the strangers were kept talking all night. When Mr. Chalmers met his friends in the morning he said, "Well, Arua, have you been at it all night?" "Oh, yes, Tamate," answered the poor fellow, who was so hoarse that he could hardly speak. "When I lay down they would come with more questions, so I'd have to get up, and explain again. But never mind: I must tell them of Jesus Christ."

When Mr. Chalmers was ready to leave the men gathered round him, begging him to sing as much as he could before going away: "No more fighting, Tamate," they said. "No more man-eating. We have heard good news, and

we shall strive for peace." "Now sing to us,"
added the women as he departed, "so that when
Tamate's face is lost we may hear his voice, and
weep that he so soon leaves us." "Tamate, come
back soon, very soon," they all cried in chorus;
"do not disappoint us, and we will bring you
everywhere upon the rivers."

The voyagers had a high sea and a strong
wind during most of the return journey, but they
arrived in safety at Port Moresby on the first of
November.

In January of the next year the teachers
and the converts from east and from west gathered at Port Moresby for a sort of thanksgiving
celebration. Services were held on New Year's
eve, and on New Year's morning there was a
meeting for prayer and praise at half-past five
o'clock. Then everybody fell to work at preparations for dinner. When everything was in
the oven the people assembled for the great
service of the occasion, and then came the feast.
The following day the teachers met quietly and
talked over their work together.

In February the John Williams appeared
once more, bringing thirteen new teachers, who
were stationed in various places. Then Mr.
Chalmers set out in the Ellengowan for another
cruise to the west, where lived the wildest but
really the noblest people of New Guinea, who

needed the youngest, strongest, bravest, and brightest teachers. They always asked for "big men." "Pick the giants for them," Mr. Chalmers said, "and they will make their mark at once."

On the way he called at many old stations, where he noticed with pleasure all signs of progress, and he visited new places also where he hoped soon to begin work. Then he went to the east on a tour of inspection, and came back much encouraged by the growth that he saw there. In this year the British Government established a protectorate over the unannexed portion of New Guinea.

In 1886 there was good news from all the stations along the coast. In August Mr. Chalmers returned to England. where he received a hearty welcome, and people thronged to hear him tell of what he had seen and heard in great, neglected New Guinea. In 1887 he was sent back by the governor of Victoria to continue his explorations. A new ship has been recently called for by the London Missionary Society, for use in New Guinea, the cost of which will be $16,000, with an additional sum of $1,500 for running expenses.

Two hundred and five teachers have gone to New Guinea from Samoa, Savage Island and Rarotonga, and from the Fiji and Loyalty

groups.   One hundred and three have died,
been killed, or had to go home on account of
the climate, but volunteers have never been
wanting to fill up the gaps.   When fifteen men
were asked for lately forty men offered themselves for the service, and the matter of which
ones should stay at home had to be decided by
lot.

There are now stations six hundred miles
along the coast.   There are seventy stations on
the mainland, and altogether there are five thousand converts.   Six languages have been reduced to writing, books have been published,
and there is a translation of the New Testament
in Motu, the speech of the trading-people on the
southeast coast.

In the meeting of Christians at Port Moresby
in 1892 the collection for missions was $37 in
money, with spears, armlets, bows and arrows,
drums, necklaces, and ornaments.   All these
things have marketable value as curios.

At one of their services one of the natives
picked up a spear and said, " This used to be
our constant companion : we dared not go to our
gardens without it ; we took it in our canoes ; we
carried it on our journeys ; we slept with it by
our sides, and we took our meals with it close at
hand ; but," he continued, holding up a copy of
the gospel, " we can now sleep safely because of

this. This book has brought us peace and protection, and we no longer require the spear."

Altogether in Polynesia there are now seven thousand missionaries and forty thousand native helpers.   There are about three hundred and fifty islands more or less fully evangelized, and the Bible, in whole or in part, has been translated into fifty languages.

The London Missionary Society asks for $80,000 with which to provide a new vessel for the South Seas, and a fourth " John Williams " is about to be sent out; so the name of the " Apostle of the Pacific " is not likely to be speedily forgotten.

And so all up and down in the South Seas have these Heroes of the Cross told the sweet old story, and still is "the good word of the kingdom " passed on from island to island.

May the One who began the work, and who has kept it on its way all through these long years, never let it falter until the multitude of isles shall be glad because the Lord reigneth, and the inhabitants thereof shall every one have heard the good tidings that a Saviour has been born into the world.

So at the last may all join in the chorus, "Glory to God in the highest, and on earth peace, good will to men."

" The Son of God goes forth to war,
   A kingly crown to gain ;
His blood-red banner streams afar ;
   Who follows in his train ?
Who best can drink his cup of woe,
   Triumphant over pain,
Who patient bears his cross below—
   He follows in His train."

www.ingramcontent.com/pod-product-compliance
Lightning Source LLC
Chambersburg PA
CBHW030104030726
47498CB00007B/2243